Wild Voices: An Anthology on Wildlife Issues

All profits from this book are to be donated to Wildlife SOS

www.wildlifesos.org

Wild Voices: An Anthology on Wildlife Issues

Compiled & Edited by David Bassett

Preface

The idea for this book arose from a desire to uncover truths and expose people to the varied wildlife issues that exist, some of which I was completely oblivious to when growing up. I had visited marine parks as a child, wanting nothing more than to become a dolphin trainer when I grew older. I would watch in amazement as these magnificent orcas and dolphins would perform trick after trick with what appeared to be smiles on their faces. I would go year on year, applauding the same creatures as they completed their four shows a day and watch in awe at the trainers who surfed on their backs and dove off of their noses.

As time passed, my love for animals only grew. I was desperate to cuddle lion cubs and ride on the backs of elephants, completely ignorant to the fact that these acts were anything but natural. In fairness, I was a child and social media was in its early stages but looking back now, I still get frustrated by the fact I was deceived by the industries who profit from and cover up the true acts that take place behind the scenes. It wasn't long though before these truths started to be uncovered, little clues here and there, which helped remove my blinkers and open my eyes to the events taking place.

Documentaries were released, photos were posted and articles were written, each of them focussed around the abuse that occurs as a result of the many animal tourist attractions operating in society. Tigers being sedated, elephants beaten and orcas going psychotic. I soaked it all in and made dramatic changes, my first, of course, being a new career choice. But the thing that shocked me the most was the ignorance that people refused to shake off. They didn't care about what they'd seen, or that's what I was made to believe. No matter how much I reposted things online or told my friends about it, they continued to visit these attractions and fund the cruelty. "You used to want to do it," they'd say. And it's true, I did aspire to check those things off my bucket list once but the difference was, I didn't know better at the time and I most definitely didn't have someone advising me otherwise.

Years later, I found my **voice**. Through teaching, I started to educate the children in my school on the issues our natural world is facing. We raised awareness and money to fund wildlife organisations, hosting a variety of wildlife visitors to help teach the future generation about how they can help to reverse the damage that has been done. I entered charity races, raising money for wildlife organisations, visited wildlife sanctuaries in Asia and used my degree in Creative Writing to write blog posts and reviews on ethical animal tourist attractions. But it wasn't enough. Not by my standards anyway. Not while I continued to encounter people as oblivious as my younger self, scrolling on my phone to find them petting tigers and riding elephants. Something had to change.

'What if I could provide these animals with a voice?' I thought. Voices that will reach out to more than the children in my class, which would draw on my skills as a writer, whilst contributing to a great cause. A novel? I didn't have the time to write one. Not as an NQT anyway. That's when the idea hit me. An anthology! A collation of short stories, from people across the world, who can help create and expose the stories I want to tell. Stories featuring wildlife issues that people are unaware of alongside vulnerable animals that need to be heard. At that moment, Wild Voices was born.

I contacted writing groups, authors and degree courses from around the world, telling them of my vision and how they could help. Writers from different backgrounds and different experiences of wildlife issues. I'll admit, I was sceptical at first. 'Who'd listen to me?' I thought, 'There are too many things like this out there.' But sure enough, it wasn't long before responses, questions and story submissions began to flood in. Before I knew it, the cover was designed and shortly after that, a charity confirmed whom I could donate the profits to. The months flew by and one year later, there it was - 30 stories and 30 Voices. Each loose end tied up. All I had to do then was make sure I got it out there and seen.

Yes, I could bore you by telling you of the process in detail, by complaining about the workload, or how many emails and edits I've endured, but I'd rather keep it short and let you know just how much of an adventure it's been– One that I know I will never forget and more importantly, one that I know will help make a difference.

I hope that this book will be read by every child who aspires to become the dolphin trainer I used to dream of being. I hope that it educates people on the events that take place behind the selfies and photo posts and that it opens their eyes to what is really happening to our wildlife today. Finally, I hope that Wild Voices inspires people to make a difference and help those that are unable to help themselves because each and every one of us are capable of making change. All we have to do is try.

David Bassett, Editor of Wild Voices.

Dedication

This book is dedicated to every animal that has suffered at the hands of the human race. Though it may not reverse the damage that has been done, I hope that this book will go on to educate people on the battles you fight each and every day and that it prevents further harm from coming to you. Your **voices** deserve to be heard and I hope that we, as the authors of this anthology, have done your stories justice.

Acknowledgements

Thank you to the following:

The thirty authors who donated their time and words to make this anthology a reality.

The extremely talented, and very close friend of mine, Venus Libido, whose artistry wrapped this book in colour and life.

To Wildlife SOS and the outstanding work they do for our world's wildlife.

And last, but not least, my friends, family and partner who have supported me through this unforgettable process.

Wildlife SOS

Wildlife SOS began because of an urgent need for urban wildlife rescues in Delhi and its environs. Snakes would get into homes, raptors and owls would be injured because of superstitious fears and as construction in Delhi went crazy, a lot of displaced wildlife from Civet cats, foxes, and jackals to monitor lizards and mongoose began to surface in farmhouses and startle people in their homes. To prevent them from being harmed, we began to assist the wildlife department by catching the animals and helping them to be rehomed in forested patches or a nearby wildlife sanctuary manned by the Forest Dept.

Our first large project was with India's "Dancing Bears" which tackled the use of illegally poached sloth bear cubs by tribals. These cubs were then sold to the Kalandar Tribe who had traditionally trained and danced the bears for centuries. What had begun as the entertainment of kings had declined into a sorry display before tourists and visitors. Although the Wildlife Act of India banned the use of wildlife for entertainment, our initial survey and report, conducted over 18 months in 68 villages, also revealed their abject poverty. There was no education, hygiene, health care or even proper habitations. Drinking water was purchased, toilets unheard of and only a dozen of them had brick homes.

What began as a project to protect sloth bears in the wild and prevent the poaching of the cubs, soon became a more holistic project in which we decided to rehabilitate the Kalandar community by educating the children and making second income earners of the women. This was so they could break their silence and speak up for themselves within their community. The men were also given seed funds, taught alternative livelihoods and encouraged to sign agreements that they would no longer earn from wildlife trade in the future.

The bears were placed in four large Rescue centres at different points in India and were given the best veterinary care, nutrition and large open natural spaces. Each bear had undergone much brutality during the training period; the baby bears would always have their canines knocked out by a pestle, the male cubs were crudely castrated with a blade (with no anaesthetic), and finally, a sharpened red-hot poker would pierce their muzzle and a thick rope be forced through it. But worst of all for the tiny cubs, their freedom would extend to the end of a four-foot rope for the rest of their lives.

Hence it was a successful conservation project that brought an end to a painfully archaic mode of entertainment. Not to mention, it actually kept the Kalandar family in poverty and was a threat to the sloth bears in the wild. By 2009, we had rescued 628 bears, rehabilitated over 3000 families and sent close to 6000 children to school. 1600 children continue to be educated, as well as the project providing them with schoolbooks, fees, tutoring help, uniforms and clothes. Everything required to make them fit into their new world. The women were helped with training in embroidery, candle making, and a large number of cottage industries, which in effect helped to stop child marriage in the community. The work with the community continues, although the trade of dancing bears has come to an end in India.

Our work with elephants began as such work often does - with one extraordinary elephant. Champa was old with abscesses and wounds, yet very affectionate. We met her one day as she groaned away with a 600kg metal howdah on her back, carrying tourists and children for rides along the highway. For nine years, we treated her in the field as her owner wouldn't let her rest until one day, her infected pus-filled foreleg gave way and Champa lay on the ground unable to move. With nothing to lose, the owner allowed us to rescue her and start treatment.

Champa recovered and lived a few years with us, during which time she taught us all how intelligent, emotionally complex and sensitive an elephant can be. More importantly, it started our work with the elephant conservation and care centre. Today, we are committed to giving captive elephants a **voice**, particularly the elephants used for begging, riding, tourism and entertainment. In recent times, there has been a huge awareness created by distressed public, filmmakers and animal welfare supporters, aghast to see the royal and magnificent Asian elephant reduced to broken down, malnourished and dehydrated work animals. In some circumstances, elephants have been made to walk for 20 hours a day in blazing heat on tarred roads, or stand endlessly at temple functions and/or marriage ceremonies.

The very process of using an elephant involves separating a calf from its family, beating it endlessly and isolating it in a kraal, tied by all four legs without mercy. These calves are fed the minimum until they learn to obey and fear their masters. And for what? For a few meaningless circus tricks, to give rides for tourists up and down forts in desert heat, or to beg with its owner for alms along India's religious sites. This is why we are now devoting ourselves to the care of suffering individual elephants that need to be retired and treated. Simultaneously, we have set up a state of the art hospital for elephants - the only one in India. We are mounting a campaign against the tourism industry promoting riding of elephants and are working hard to have circus elephants rehabilitated and the use of elephants for begging reduced, if not phased out as fast as possible.

It's a long and hard task we have set ourselves because tradition and culture is hard to challenge, but we are also fuelled by the desire to protect the twenty to twenty-two thousand elephants left in the wild. They should remain out of captivity with their corridors protected and their right to exist inviolate. India is the last stronghold of Asian elephants in the wild and we will do what we can to keep these elephants safe.

Geeta Seshamani, Co-Founder of Wildlife SOS.

Hatched

Turtles never really stop being eggs. We may look different once we've split our casing and pushed our way out through its cracks, but our fate remains the same as any other egg. We have shells to shield our gooey centers and we hold hope, though it sounds overly optimistic, that one day we might grow into more solid forms. Unfortunately, the sands that our mothers once buried us beneath now resemble that of a human's cooking pan – one that has made our fight for life that little bit more difficult. We're on an ever-changing menu and we are the meal.

Follow the light we are born to believe. Follow the light to remain a yolk. Sounds easy enough, doesn't it? I pop my head out from the nest and glance around to see dozens, no hundreds of other yolks doing the same. A burning light blazes down and its rays quickly begin to cook our little scalps. We must hurry! Like an army's tiny soldiers, we crawl our way into the light, towards the sea, but it's not long before my vision begins to blur. I slow. My joints – heavy. Maybe I should take a break? Something tells me I'm not supposed to, but with each step I feel my skin turn crisper. My goo – cooking. Not to mention, I can see plenty of my siblings doing the same through my squinting eyes. They turn darker, blacker. What am I thinking? I can't rest! But I can't fight the heat either. My eyes slowly surrender to it and the smell of sizzling yolk fills my nostrils. FRIED.

Follow the light we are born to believe. Follow the light to remain a yolk. Sounds easy enough, doesn't it? A glimmering, white light rests above the crashing waves, only this time, a cool wind tickles my face and the sand beneath my flippers feels cold, almost damp. Something tells me we stand more of a chance under the blanket of night. We must waste no time and make a dash for it. As we scurry towards the frothing waves, silhouettes eclipse the moon's light. Go faster! Must go faster! But it's not long before I see my brothers and sisters lifted from beside me. Each one of them pecked off - tiny morsels for the swooping shadows. I scuttle my fastest until I can taste the salt of the sea, so fast that I begin to fly, soaring up above the sands. My tiny flippers continue to flap, but it's useless. I sink further down into a cramped pipe and away from the light of the moon. A new light engulfs my eyes. POACHED.

Follow the light we are born to believe. Follow the light to remain a yolk. Sounds easy enough, doesn't it? There's a new light on these sands. Its orange glow hums a soothing song. It calls to us. It's tranquil. Surely it's the way? Engrossed in its melody, we pursue it, but it's not long before the sand under our stomachs solidifies. The grains fade away and the blasts of the crashing waves become fainter, muffled by the roars of monsters. They whizz past us in different directions, rolling on four wheels and separating us from the orange lights. The bravest of us try their luck first, slipping on the concrete path and spinning on their shells belly-up as larger metal monsters zoom past. It's a trick! There is no ocean here! Splats and squelches echo the road as my fellow yolks are mushed in the pan but before I can retreat to the shore, I too am swept onto my back. Helpless and fragile like every other yolk, never to escape the menu that determines our fate.

I was going to ask how you humans like your eggs, but it's pretty clear from what I can see. You like us SCRAMBLED.

David Bassett, Primary School Teacher & Wild Voices Creator, Hampshire.

The People of the Forest

This was our forest once.

Sorrow wrenches her throat as my mother recalls days of dense vegetation, abundant fruit and a life which seems so different to ours. Her eyes used to cloud when she'd think back to before we were born, but strangely now a permanent mist covers those once-dark bulbs; a mist that's descended over the past few months, coinciding with a gradual sagging of her skin and the thinning of her hair.

Dewi notices these things and tells me when we're out of mum's earshot.

Dewi's my twin sister.

Dewi worries a lot.

I try to ignore it but I can't help but see the things which Dewi notices. Mum's emaciated body is slumped against the trunk of our latest home. She struggled to build our last nest which meant her hair is still soaked from curling over us to offer protection from the tiny daggers which pummelled down from above.

This morning brings new terrifying sounds which echo through the jungle. I need to stay brave for my sister. But when a potential home tumbles and sends an ear-splitting crack through the forest, I can't help but join Dewi in her jolt of panic. Adrenaline floods my muscles and my instant reaction is to grab my sister and bolt.

How can mum just sit there, barely raising her brow?

We haven't found sustenance for days and fatigue is clearly setting in. Dewi clings to mum and we plead with her to swing away from whatever it is that's making that chugging, spluttering racket. Birds are taking flight around us and the forest is alive with the sounds and smells of terror.

Still mum doesn't move. We need her to move. Why won't she move?

It's the middle of the day but the skies turn grey around us. I've never seen so many birds ascend at once. Heaven takes on the sounds of the forest. Terrified squawks of the birds that take refuge in the world above us hammer at my eardrums.

Those without wings crash through the undergrowth – a dizzy frenzy of creatures large and small; all instincts of their place in the

3

natural order forgotten as panic takes over. My kind don't have many predators that I know of; but in this moment, everything feels hunted.

Mum casts those clouded eyes downwards and sees the havoc below but still doesn't move. Dewi and I can't leave without her. All we can do is cling to that once-cushioned skin and try to shut out the panic around us.

We're not moving but the explosions creep closer and closer, accompanied by calls, hollers and chattering that are alien to me.

Time slips and they're below us. This new predator has seen us. They're pointing up at us, but still mum doesn't move. Her wasted muscles barely flinch as we cling to her, eyes locked on each other, willing her into action. Dewi's eyes have become deep caverns of fear. I try to feign bravery but am sure my unblinking eyes give me away.

The creatures below keep pointing and hollering - unnatural calls which sound like no ape I've heard before. The monster that's creating that rhythmic chugging din has stopped directly below our temporary home. I can see its clouded breath pumping out but can't see its eyes. One of the apes holds this growling beast with both hands. Presumably it's trained to follow his command.

More pointing. More hollering.

And then the ape that's holding the spluttering creature looks down at a strap on his wrist and shakes his head. He pushes the monster forward until it connects with the base of our home.

The world vibrates and then cracks below us. Suddenly, we're falling. My heart thunders out of my chest and Dewi shrieks. Her screams ring through me. We need to flee.

We crash into the forest floor; dust billowing around us. Mum just managed to hold on to the branches as we fell and now she stands, Dewi still clinging to her. She pushes me behind her and bares her teeth at the creatures which face off against us.

We have to run. But Dewi won't let go. Her hands are frozen around mum's protruding skeleton.

I run, find a place to hide and look back at the aftermath of the fall, face buried from the shame of leaving them. Mum is no match for these apes with their sticks.

A final cry, then mum's body goes limp beneath the savage crowd.

4

The apes prise Dewi's hands off of mum's body and force her tiny frame into a wooden box on the back of a huge growling monster. Punctuated calls of "sell", "pet" and "dollars" erupt from the apes' mouths. Their communications sound so strange to my ears.

Mum's limp, lifeless body lies curled next to Dewi; dumped with no thoughts of the impact of the scene on my sister. Her dignity in life is disregarded and she is awarded none in death.

Shame and sadness overwhelm me as the monster moves away. Those terrified cavernous eyes stare back at me through the bars of Dewi's box as she slowly gets taken.

Our eyes stay locked until she's out of sight and then, for the first time in my life, I'm alone.

These apes have destroyed my home, my family and my future.

Years ago they named us Orangutans - The People of the Forest.

I guess they've decided that we no longer matter.

This shell of the forest is theirs now.

Christopher Moore, Chartered Accountant, Bristol.

Who Is the Loser?

She crouched low in the grass, downwind, eyes focused straight ahead, waiting for the moment to spring, unaware of the danger to her right, unseen, camouflaged in a bind many feet away.

A few silent steps forward – then the burst of speed toward the prey. Only to be crumpled with one shot.

Mardie Schroeder, author of *Go West for Luck Go West for Love*, USA.

The Last Buck

PART 1

He was a buck, noble and strong. His brown hide glistened in the midday sun. His antlers were tall and proud, stretching forth like the branches of a healthy tree. His face was long, narrow, nose wide, eyes dark and alert, legs strong and powerful. His back was straight and broad. With every step, the muscles of his frame tightened and released, magnificent under his thick hide. Each curious sound caused him to stand erect, abrupt and aware, long ears moving front to back as he cautiously listened into the wind. His nose was damp and shimmered with moisture while his nostrils flared in and out as he tested the air, ever alert. When he would bow his head to graze, the tall antlers seemed to thrust forward like spears of ancient warfare.

The buck appeared indeed a celestial embodiment of the forest's royalty, and it was with each dignified step that all of nature hushed in coveted admiration. He was regal, graceful, and stoic. It was as if the trees did bow their branches to have him in their presence. His hooves left deep impressions in the earth as he moved along the soft ground. His movements were purposeful, even forceful, but each step was slow, delicate, and carefully placed. Given the moment to flee, the buck was quick, sharp, and agile. Every bound was as though he had taken flight, each crash upon the ground furious and rapid. As he soared through the air, the muscles beneath his skin protruded with the strength of his escape; his head turned slightly downward as he thrust his antlers forward into the air, his four powerful legs rising and falling with each gargantuan leap.

When he lay upon the ground that fateful day, panting, tongue protruding from his mouth, his eyes wild, it would have made even the most insensitive creature stop and look with remorse upon his enviable frame. He had put on a gallant display of elegance and cunning as he fled; yet, the bullet had found him nonetheless, and in an instant had torn through the thick hide, radiant now with the sweat of his labors.

In a haunted shriek, the buck cried out as the bullet pierced his chest, blood spilling across his legs and neck as his body plummeted to the ground. The birds, high above in their lookouts, recoiled, but with curious eye. For a moment, all was silent, until the sound of the trees swaying, their leaves chattering in the wind, lamented the fall of the noble buck. The smell of earth filled his nostrils, which were now enlarged and moving slowly as his breath became more shallow. In his pain, he did not move, but panted with belabored breath. His eyes jut out far beyond his head, opened wide, staring into the sky, almost fearful.

Then, the buck's breathing stopped; his brown hide losing its glisten in an instant. The wild eyes became like glass, empty and shallow. The antlers protruded no more, but lay like dead branches against the earth. The muscles within his body became loose, their strength gone, his face twisted and bloody. As his body lay upon the ground, the trees once again bowed their branches, but to mourn the passing of such a regal creature as he.

PART 2

It was the quivering rush of the hunt that enthralled me as I kept pace with him. He was unique, alone, undoubtedly the last of his kind. His majestic head looking down upon my parlour would easily draw the envy of my varied and distinguished guests. I had toiled for many days, endured countless dangers, and trekked an endless path to find him. He was mine and I deserved him. If I did not take him in that moment, that second of opportunity which had finally arrived, then surely some other person would. Could they appreciate him the way that I did, or would his gallantry remain hidden in the dark corridors of some less worthy trophy hall?

Perhaps some small part of me contemplated his end, his untimely demise, but it was not I who had hunted his species to this brink, where now I encountered him. I was merely one part of his story, just as he was the culmination of years past. He had survived the slaughter and he was now here before me, his life hanging in the precarious balance of my actions. Yet, as the buck took flight, and as I drew in my breath to hold my rifle (and my resolve) steady, my mind wandered to contemplate that which I was about to extinguish. Just a flash of conscious – to that creature which would be my prey and through which I would find my glory. My eyes burned with excitement.

A pause.

Steady now, another breath in.

It was my moment. I must seize opportunity as it revealed itself. I must take the trophy for my own. I was not responsible for the buck's forefathers' eternal demise, and my grandchildren would know of the buck's valiant struggle before the game board of fate was set in my favour. If they were to ask, I would admit to this deed, albeit illegal and dangerous, but perhaps they would believe my reasons. Understand them even. Perhaps they would not question the buck's fate and we would speak no more of the subject. One day, the buck would appear in an encyclopedia of extinct species, and so I would have also made history. I would tell my grandchildren, the choice was plain, and perhaps they would not loathe me long for taking this part of their future. Perhaps they would understand that I was simply living in my moment. It was mine, not theirs. For what could they care for such a buck, and would they truly mourn his passing?

Sara K. Phillips, Environmental and Natural Resources Attorney, Bangkok.

The Loneliness of the Long Distance Panda

There were no two ways about it, he clunked when he walked. It was the near hind that was causing the problem. He'd noticed it days ago, soon after crossing the Bering Strait, some eighty-five relentless kilometers of icy saltwater. Pad, pad, pad clunk! Pad, pad, pad, clunk. Yes, definitely the hip. Too much exercise and way too much salt water.

He'd not been made for this kind of travel, just a little gentle shuffling between bamboo groves, avoiding too many ups and downs. He'd heard them talking about him in the lab before he was released. A bear, they'd called him, Ailuropoda melanoleuca, black and white cat-foot, a living fossil. They said his closest ursine relative was the Spectacled Bear of South America, Tremarctos ornatus. He'd checked his GPS, still functioning after all this time, and pondered in the manner of his kind. China to South America was a long walk for a panda, but he could do it if he had to.

It had been many years since he'd walked out of the Qinling Mountains in the hilly Shanxi Province and set off to find more of his kind, but though he'd walked north through China to Siberia, he'd found no organic creature larger than a cockroach and no one like himself. He didn't know what had happened to his makers, but it must have happened a long time ago. They'd gone the way of the panda at last.

Back in the early 21st Century, the International Union for Conservation of Nature had declared his species as endangered and conservation reliant, but not followed through until it was too late. Maybe they'd thought it enough that the giant panda genome had been sequenced in 2009, but it took more than that to keep a whole species viable. It took bamboo and more bamboo and the resources shrank each year.

That's when they'd made him and others like him. Giant pandas, able to live in the wild on fresh air – a sop to national pride. Something for the tourists to gawp at, perfect in all respects, on the outside at least. On the inside, however, their hearts were tiny fusion reactors, their skeletons foam-metal, their joints ceramic, and their muscles, skin and fur woven from various polymers.

He could access his internal clock if he really wanted to and find out how long it had been since the others ceased to function. He was the last of his kind, and pretty soon he'd be unable to walk. Pad, pad, pad-clunk! What would happen then? He imagined himself stranded in this land of glaciers. How long would it take for his fuel cell to run down? Too long. He wondered if it was possible for a creature like him to go mad.

Alaska's broken coastline caused him detour after detour and he stopped checking his clock, fearful of seeing years pass while he relentlessly plodded south. Always south. Pad, pad, pad-clunk through Alaska and British Columbia until the pad, pad, pad-clunk became pad, pad, clank-clunk.

He had to skirt an active volcano where Seattle used to be. Its rumbling and occasional belch of acrid smoke set off his alarm systems and the volcanic grit irritated his retractable claw beds, causing him delays for cleaning and maintenance. Pad, pad, clank-clunk became pad, pad, clank-drag and he was grateful when he reached the benign forests of Oregon.

He was resting his rear hind servo when he heard a whine above him and felt the sudden tug of an antigrav hauler. He was whisked up to a laboratory in the sky. Surprise wasn't one of his inbuilt emotions and he knew all about laboratories, even alien ones, so he settled down feeling only mild curiosity. They shot him with a cryo-anaesthetic that might have worked if he'd been organic, or might have killed him, since the aliens, themselves crystalline blobs, seemed to know so little of earth-based physiology that they couldn't tell the difference between biological and mechanical. At least they didn't seem interested in taking him apart to see how he worked.

He lay awake for the ninety years it took for their ark ship to return home, grateful that the enforced rest gave his depleted nanites time to repair most of the damage to his hip joints. Occasionally he would open one eye and watch the aliens at work, gleaning an understanding of their communication system, a mixture of audible sounds and electronic impulses. They never seemed to figure out his recorded system responses, though, which were in Mandarin.

14

In the alien zoo, they gave him a huge enclosure that replicated the forest they'd found him in exactly, and put up a communication repeater that he deciphered as "Dominant species of Planet 40698-C." He shrugged and methodically deleted his GPS database to make room for new information, then, set off in a southerly direction. Pad, pad, pad-clink.

He found her on the fourth day, staring, round-eyed and hopeful from the lower branches of a tall tree. He'd walked up one side of the earth and back down again to find another of his kind, and here she was, halfway round the galaxy in an alien zoo. From her black coat to her lighter eye markings, she was a prime example of the Spectacled Bear of South America. He dipped his head in acknowledgement and she dipped hers in return. She climbed down her tree and walked towards him shyly. The faint sound of her servos, pad-clunk, pad, pad, drifted towards him and it made his little fusion reactor glad within his breast.

Jacey Bedford, Author, Yorkshire.

The Unseen

The object fell from the sky and hit the water, throwing ripples into my resting-place in the hollow of a small rock. I adjusted my fins and flicked my tail to steady myself. I was anxious not to be seen as two humans leaned over the stream. Another missile flew from the hand of one intruder, this time catching in the crevice between two rocks, blocking my usual path and my right of passage.

Polly Hartley, Writer, Birmingham.

The Animal Lover

I love animals. Chickens, turkeys, ducks, pheasants, grouse, geese, partridges, rabbits, goats, lambs, fish, shellfish, insects, larvae, grubs, deer, cattle, pigs – I'll eat them all. Pigeons and squirrels are really tasty in a pie if you can trap them without getting arrested. Woodpigeon's kind of Victorian. I also like elks, moose and buffalo as pemmican bases. I once had dog and cat meat as a novelty dish. Horse meat's delicious too – full of lean protein. A great post-workout snack. As for sheeps' eyes – they're sort of like grapes. I like to take a pocketful with me when I go out for the day. I once tried deep-fried pinky-mice that were on sale in an outdoor market. They're a bit like cocktail sausages.

Hunting, now there's a pastime. Nothing like bringing home something you caught with your bare hands. I have a gun. It's called Lancelot. I went on a rug-making course last year, since I was bringing home so many skins. Bears and wolves mostly. The heads and tails are mounted on my wall. I also had a couple of oilskins made into coats after I went sealing Up North. Oh, and you can thank the dolphins for these lovely lamps. Renewable oil – just imagine! The amount I save on mains electricity...

I've even got some fur coats made of big cat skins, and one from a polar bear – although that was more a case of self-defence. I've got him stuffed. He's on display in my living room if you're interested? Oh, and see that piano? I caught the keys. Tried to donate the bones to the museum but they said they had enough already.

Do you want to see my collection of pressed butterflies? It's pushing one thousand now. I'm so proud of it – I've got nearly every species. I take the net out every summer. And look – here's my collection of rare birds' eggs. You've got to be good at climbing for that. See those tiny holes? That's where I blow the yolk out so they don't stink up the place. You have to go early in the year so it's not a great big chick inside it, of course.

Yes – I just love animals!

Catherine Spark, PhD in Creative Writing, Scotland.

Sudan's Last Gift

This was the end of everything. The end of a lifetime learning about survival, to save something that should never, never have been endangered.

The place was enclosed, but there has never been any risk with Sudan. A gentle beast, he had always been a favourite. But today, amongst the yellowed grass, there was loss. It hung heavy on the air, wrapping its dry warmth around them, cradling them in sadness. Rangers had come to say goodbye to the last Northern White Rhino male in existence. It was the end of an age of trying to get him to breed, to eke out a faint glimmer of hope for the ailing species - Sudan had tried to do his duty in earlier years and two females remained: his daughter and grand-daughter. A family, clinging on to survival after countless years of persecution by hunters. Such is the nature of the most dangerous of species in the arid African plains. Not the mighty four legged predators, the ferocious hunters of the Masai Mara; it's the human scourge that destroys.

Stunned, the park rangers had come to pay their last respects. Sudan was old, there was no denying, 45 is a great age for a rhino, but that didn't make the parting any easier. He stood breathing torturously, the great cavern of his chest undulated with an effort that only portended one thing. The rangers were powerless to stop time. Sudan's fate, and that of the Northern White Rhino, had been written in indelible ink.

*

My breath is coming in gasps, the effort herculean. I am sure it is time soon to pass on. Yet why are my humans looking so sad? It's time to give up my old, leathery, tough body and take on the air, into my tissue. I have given my all. It's time to go. I'm tired. I need rest. Don't they understand that? I turn my dense head with the effort of death towards those strange beings I have called my friends for so long.

"Don't worry about me," I want to say.

21

I will it to them, like telepathy. To Angelo, my closest companion, I want to gift peace. It's what he deserves, what he needs.

"Don't worry about me. I go to rest. I go to watch and I go to relief.

It's you, Mpenzi wangu. For you, you must toil. Your work is not done. It is not time for you to stop.

"Let me go, now."

*

Today, the Conservatory has lost one battle, a serious one for this species, but not all is wasted. Before Sudan died, he bequeathed them a last gift – his seed - to bring life where death preceded.

A faint chance for the Northern White Rhino to live on, despite the odds.

Angela Brown, English Teacher, England.

'*Garuhurooboo, gruhuh, garoo, garoo!*' The deep throaty growl rose from the furry mass.

'*Wah-hah-do-you-doo, what'll-ye-do, what'll-ye-do, what'll-ye-do,*' was a falling-twirling squeak from above, which he thought he should perhaps pay regard to.

He looked out through his flopping fur and began shuffling backwards from the long shining yellow beak hanging down from the branch above, where each side of the gleaming iridescent green hunch of feathers was a clutching orange claw.

A swishing, shuffling wound itself enquiringly around Bonobo's feet and a small head rose to show a sharp dark V between and above the two piercing eyes. The jagged dark mark shot down and along the flexing, curving, narrow back. Below the V-divided eyes, a red forked flashing tongue dispensed regular hisses, which punctuated meaning.

'*Ssss-let's-seeee, ssss-let's-seeee, who's to be, who's to be, follow me, follow me,*' it told him as it wound under a spreading patch of dark green foliage.

Bonobo could hear a rhythmic beat, a loud roaring sound, which increased as some other higher floating melody rose through the trees. His paws extended and contracted as he wondered what to do. Who else was there? Again, above him, he heard the twirling squeak and then there was a roaring flutter as wide wings opened and the cry of '*what'll-ye-do, what'll-ye-do, what'll-ye-do,*' lifted skywards, following the round sound and the melody.

Bonobo wasn't sure. He'd only woken yesterday from a deep slumber and hadn't fully come back to life. But echoing in his head was the hissing, '*sss-let's-seee* and *follow me.*'

He looked both ways and then decided. He lumbered off and dived through the green foliage.

As the beat became louder, he was aware of another vibration from the ground and he was puzzled. What could be causing it? It followed the same beat, or a little faster. Suddenly, he found himself between the trees on the edge of a brightly lit clearing and stood amazed. Tight skins stretched over hollowed trunks were being beaten with large pieces of varnished wood: the familiar shapes of

23

rifle stocks. Animals of all shapes and sizes were moving rhythmically together, their paws and hooves causing the ground to joyously vibrate.

This was what they had all been waiting for in the forest. The humans had found the right way, now they had detached those barrels and found a better use for the stocks. In fact they were turning out to be pretty good drummers in the dance of life.

Celia Wallis, Designer & Builder, Birmingham.

Sound Waves

Ana never liked the term scientist. It felt too synthetic, too sterile. Spiritless.

The science secured her funding and for the first three years of her tenure, she submitted her findings and the trustees interpreted them. Everyone heard exactly what they wanted to hear: human activity was becoming more sustainable. Ecosystems adapted. Organisms survived.

Ana's data satisfied the swelling concern of campaign groups, gently drowning the issues as surely as the incoming tide submerges the shore.

***

The yellow line on the blue-green screen of Ana's second-hand SONUS receiver oscillated erratically. 12 nautical miles away, a hydrophone wrestled for stability in wake and white water. Ana traced the containership's engine resonating on another hydrophone floating a further 12 miles away. Simultaneously, she recorded the accompanying vocalisations of a finback over even vaster distances. Compressing the time and raising the pitch before playback made it easier to hear. A sharp, staccato pulse fell immediately from 36 hertz to 23, registering at 186 decibels, the aquatic equivalent of a rocket launch. It wasn't so much a crescendo as a momentary release of sound that expands out from itself, getting relatively louder and lower, like the syncopated spasm of air exploding in the bell of a muted tuba.

***

The university expanded her laboratory and invested in equipment. Her undergraduate assistant, Alda, become a salaried intern. Ana gave interviews to news outlets: they photographed her barefoot on a tropical beach observing turtles. Her social media handle was attached to issues from rising sea levels to the managing of seabird populations. Then she published a paper that caused a tidal wave and her career capsized.

25

Listing dangerously, Ana held onto the ship's wheel so tightly that the tiller, wrenched in opposite directions, snapped. To starboard, a slender fin sliced the surface; the great mass of body hidden, iceberg-like, threatening to overturn her boat with every graceful sweep of its fluke. Balancing heavily on her port hull, the Hlysnan - a retired racing yacht that Ana had reconditioned - eventually regained a balanced keel and her sails filled with a dense artic wind. She steered leeward, hoping to catch a run and put some distance between herself and the world's second-largest whale. Upwind and retreating, the finback spouted its tall, elegant spray, glittering white in the sunlight as if in apology. Ana's gaze followed the gentle grey arch of its dorsal ridge rolling like the Downs caught in dawn's mist as it vaulted in silver silence.

***

A year ago, neither her yacht or reputation were seaworthy, but Ana had been secretly financing her own research and had syphoned small sums off her grants in order to prove that whales were capable of producing a wide range of sophisticated vocalisations that might be said to resemble song.

Ana believed that whales sang purely for the joy of singing. Despite the fact that everything she had learned about the natural world suggested that there was an evolutionary explanation for even the most bizarre behaviours, she was convinced that certain complex species were creative creatures.

So far, given the need to disguise her research, Ana focused on monitoring ambient noise in seas with high volumes of commercial shipping and areas of coastline with a high proportion of motorised craft. She had already shown that the feeding habits of dolphins were affected by their ability to navigate this new marine soundscape. Now independent, Ana explored the aesthetics of whale song and how it was being silenced by man-made noises. She noticed that instead of the melodious compositions that carried hundreds of miles, amplified by oceanic gyres performing across continental shelves, the whales she now studied showed a

26

discordant period of soundlessness punctuated by signals of distress.

***

A trawler, its engine the splutter of a drunken seafarer, reported a vessel drifting in open sea. The captain described to the coastguard rigging that hung slack and sails that lay in a crumpled pile on the deck. He was suspicious, as sailors are, of the cruciform silhouette of the skeleton mast, boom and spinnaker pole. Identifying the Hlysnan, the captain hauled close, confirmed coordinates and then lowered a dingy for two of his crew.

A finback, erupting like a fluid earthquake, burst beneath the hull as the dingy approached. Spume boiled in a freezing cloud and they were unbalanced by aftershocks of surf. Breaching, it spat from its blowhole a hiss of salt-soaked air and dived, raising its fluke in protest.

The captain cut the engines. The yacht and dingy, like parasitic pilot fish, buoyed in quiet synchronisation with the trawler. Drifting closer, one fisherman caught the rail, anchoring the two small boats, while the second fisherman threw a line to the trawler and tugged them together to form a helpless raft.

The finback floated listlessly, its sad strain recording on the instruments inside the cabin where Ana lay unresponsive. A fisherman shook her to sense and spoke softly.

"Shh," she whispered. Her voice was sail-cloth coarse, like a breathless wind after a storm.

***

Watching from a private research vessel, crowd-funded to monitor North Atlantic plastic, a tug towed the Hlysnan past the breakwater and Alda recalled the time when Ana first exposed her confidential research: "Our oceans will survive," Ana hypothesised, "but in silencing its song, we are destroying its soul."

Reporters, casting their lines, tried to bait the Harbour Master. Cameras flashed like gulls dive-bombing crab crates. Ana, pallid with dehydration and hypothermia, was hauled up as if she were

27

the catch of the day and loaded into the ambulance. The Hlysnan was hoisted into a dry dock and left to drip.

Buttoning her lab coat, Alda picked up a pair of Nitrile gloves and some sample bags and walked across the pontoon towards to the beached Hlysnan. Inside, she jostled with the salvaging officials requesting access. Convincingly, Alda asked permission to recover scientific apparatus on behalf of the university. She bagged Ana's laptop, recording equipment and notebooks quickly, leaving the rest to wreckage.

Alexander Dawson, Writer, United Kingdom.

Scraps

Fifty miles and a bag thrown over a hedge, the top untied for humanity... Once a loved pet, paraded for visitors in a diamond collar, now I live feral beside the motorway on scraps discarded by travellers. At night, they see only the glow of two emeralds.

Simon Bullock, History Student, Birmingham.

A World without Honeybees

The creepiest looking creature Lily had ever seen, was suddenly a three meter hologram in the front of the classroom. While she knew it wasn't real, as Mr. Clifton spun the projection for the students to see all dimensions of the beast, she flinched.

It was mainly yellow and black, with two antennae, a hairy body, and eyes of which Lily had never seen before on this planet. Its six scrawny legs, each with spiny feet, didn't look strong enough to withstand the weight of the monster's body. There were two plastic-like wings, which must have meant flight was the main mode of transportation it used.

"This was a honeybee, *Apis mellifera*."

Murmurs filled the room, trying to figure out what either the word "honey" or "bee" could mean.

"What did it do?" A student in the front asked.

"And why is it so massive?" Another contributed.

"I made this larger for you to see the intricacies of the insect. Actual size was more between five and fifteen millimeters." Mr. Clifton tapped something on his tablet, which caused the hologram to shrink to actual size. "Like this."

Lily barely recognized it from her seat as the same being as before.

"What honeybees did, seemed simple, but was the foundation for how most of the living things on earth endured. They did something called *pollination*. Pollination was vital for roughly a third of the plants that lived back in the early 2100s. Those plants produced many, now extinct, fruits, vegetables, and nuts. When the bees were no longer around, this vegetation ceased to be able to thrive, which had a detrimental ripple effect up the food chain. Animals which survived primarily on this food source, died off shortly afterwards. The creatures that preyed off those primary consumers, starved next. We don't even know all of the species that were lost. We do know that there was a major crash in the human population as well, down from what they thought was the carrying capacity of the world. This was great at first, getting the masses down to a respectable amount once again. Little did they know, that so many more people could live once we stopped relying solely on organic food resources. People used to think that mankind would not survive without the honeybee. They underestimated our ingenuity." Mr. Clifton turned the hologram off, but the image was seared into Lily's brain.

"How did we bounce back from the population crash?"

"We realized that the main reason we were eating the food the bees were pollinating, was for the nutrition. All that is, are molecules. These are made from atoms, which still exist, even without the bees. Scientists learned a long time ago how to manipulate the smallest units of matter to be arranged how they would like. This is why your meals have been fortified with your complete nutrients for the day. No matter what you choose to eat, it's as nutritious as anything else. Once we learned to modify the molecules within the food, the population, unfortunately, started to spike more quickly than before the honeybees died."

"Why did the bees die off?"

"Mainly stupidity. On our part, not theirs. We knew their populations were struggling for at least a century. Bee habitats were continuously being taken over by areas that were not conducive to getting them the best nutrition. That shortened their lives. The areas that should have been viable, were poisoned by manmade chemicals. People were aware of these issues, but refused to accept that they were the direct cause of the population decline. They could have protected the environments, and stopped using the poisons. Instead, they had a 'prove it to me' attitude, thinking that what they were doing wasn't a problem. Of course, there were other contributing factors in the ultimate demise of the honeybee, but the largest ones were able to be altered if people had chosen to step up."

Lily raised her hand, waiting to be acknowledged before speaking. "Mr. Clifton, do you think if the honeybee was still around, society may not be run by the government?"

"It's definitely a strong theory. Once people were not able to grow their own food, as honeybees allowed, the need for nutrition to be regulated had to be in the hands of someone. As the one, all controlling government system was being established in the 2300s, standardizing food sources was on their agenda. Now, if they didn't have the need to command our diets, would they still have formed?

Possibly. Likely. No one can know for sure. I'm sending you the next chapter to read, on how the government came to control what we eat, and what that does for us."

Just as Mr. Clifton entered something on his tablet, a new message appeared on Lily's personal screen. "New Assignment: Reading and Closure Questions." She lightly tapped on the cool glass screen of her tablet, which opened the chapter. She intently began to read.

Katie Vandrilla, High School Chemistry Teacher, USA.

Silent Watcher

There once was a silent watcher, who slid amongst the shadows of the trees. So old, so silent, and so long forgotten. Like lost words, she had all but disappeared - touching the tips of tongues, but never alighting long enough to become whole. Ancient. Powerful. Majestic. Invisible creature.

She had heard the tales of the wolf and the fox, of the bear and the boar. She had in fact, shared her home with them, though little did they know it. She had seen the wolf who had tricked the girl and swallowed her whole; she had known the man who had traded his skin for the fur of the mighty bear; she had met the too clever fox that had his very tail stolen as he and the other woodland animals blinded the skinner; she had heard the might of the boar as he crashed through the undergrowth, gouging any hunter that sought him there. She had listened as the tales were told to children late at night; told as warnings and as lessons to be learned of the power of wild creatures - but not once did she hear her own name spoken.

She had thought that it was her curse to slip into this otherworldly land between night and day; a curse to punish her for her secret and silent ways, for her ability to disappear into the shadow and dappled light of the forest floor. But no, centuries had passed, and with them her brothers and sisters came to join her in her silent waiting. The bear. The boar. The wolf. The beaver. The white tail. There were so many of them now that their silence was deafening. A vigil. Waiting to be made whole again. Some, whose names were still spoken by the Two Feet children, were more solid than she - more substantial - more alert. But she had almost given up waiting, watching.

She could not remember how long it had been since her pads had touched the dew-dampened earth of the forest floor; since the summer sun had warmed her fur; since her whiskers had felt the electricity of the storms. How long had it been since she last sunk her teeth into the still, warm flesh of the roe deer? She was almost ready to accept her fate of infinite invisibility. Almost ready to be forgotten to time. Almost.

It happened one day that her brother, the beaver, was made flesh again. She would not have believed it if she hadn't seen it with her own eyes. It was the Two Feet - the very creatures that had taken her and her siblings from this world of living and breathing and cast them into this silent, endless slumber of waiting. They had returned him to the earth. Once more he could slip into the cool waters and taste it's fresh, sweet, wetness for himself. She felt joy at the sight of him, but it was accompanied - as it often is - by such profound sadness of her own. Once again she felt the bitter jolt of her nothingness in this land that she had called home - made all the more unbearable by the beaver slapping his tail on the water's surface. Hope can be a terrible thing.

To hope is to wish for the impossible; to long for the unrealistic; it is to believe in magic. But what was she if she was not made of magic? The Two Feet of today were not the Two Feet of her yesteryear; perhaps there was hope to have.

It was not just the beaver. The goshawk and the white tail too had found their way back to solid form with the help of the Two Feet. But she was hesitant. Her little sister, the wildcat - she was fading in and out of form and shadow. Once so bold to roam across every corner of this island home of theirs, now she slunk and hid in only the most unreachable wilderness - clinging on with literal tooth and claw. But for all that, she was still real, still solid, still whole - if a little less like a Scottish tiger and a little more like a Two Feet pet - she was still alive! She had watched as the Two Feet had found ways to bring her sister more solidly back into this world so that she might hunt and stalk and bathe in the evening sunlight. Oh to stalk and hunt... how her mouth watered at the thought of the many, many deer that now roamed through her forgotten territory!

The sight of that beaver's tail stayed with her - all the more poignant for it's useless act - to warn others of predators that no longer existed in this home of theirs. Perhaps that's what she needed. Not a tail, but a tale! One for the Two Feet to tell to their children - to speak of her beauty and her prowess; of her power and her stealth!

But to ask for the Two Feet to tell her tale, she must first be seen. She must come out of the shade and the shadow, remove herself from the cool dappled light of the trees and the twilight darkness of the forest. She must shed her coat of invisibility and say, "See me, for I am Lynx! I am creature of shadow and keeper of secrets. I am hunter of deer and mother of kit. My heart still beats and my blood still flows within these forests. Let me breathe again!"

Perhaps it was time. Time to stop being the Silent Watcher. Time to be made whole again.

Suzee Gibson, Historical Interpreter, Scotland.

Overpopulation

The fox crept low, orange flashing through the deep undergrowth of the woods. She felt her belly grumble, and knew it wouldn't be satisfied tonight. She was saving whatever she managed to scavenge for something far more special; her cubs. Three in all, the other two hadn't made it. They were just starting to wrestle, and brought chaos into her den, but she loved them unequivocally.

It was quiet these days, not many animals left. As new building sites sprang up on either side of the now sparse woodland, a lot of wildlife left, or simply weren't seen again. The fox never left though, she felt drawn to the place she was born and intended to rear her kits there too, until they were old enough to leave.

It was to the buildings she now headed. Sunlight through dappled leaves turned to darkness, the temperature dropping as the trees hummed their melancholy tune. She could tell by the thud and roll of wheels on tarmac that it was bin collection day. And she knew this meant she could bring her cubs home more than a meagre mouthful of overripe berries. The rabbits had left with the growth of the second building site, after it was built directly on top of the majority of burrows.

Weaving through the tangles of blackberry bushes and following her nose, ignoring the gentle tug of burrs catching on her tail, she stopped by the edge of the forest, peering out from between two conifers at the house cast in semi-shadow. The sun had almost set, the last watery light disappearing behind the hills to the west. This meant her cubs would soon be waking, if they weren't already, and they were prone to wander. She had to get back soon. Casting her large hazel eyes over the gargantuan, slightly terrifying shadow of brick and mortar, she spotted the bin near the door. She almost missed it.

Quietly does it, she nimbly leapt over the boundary separating manicured lawn to dense forestry. The bin, however, was too tall, the lid closed too tightly. No food to be found, not even a crumb. The next garden across was different to how it used to be. Where it was once a flat plain, now a huge wooden wall had been erected, slatted and smelling of chemicals. Trying to dig her way underneath with her claws, she came across nothing but smooth cold stone, her dewclaw catching on the surface. She gave a whine of frustration, hot air blowing through her nostrils in a huff. Berries it was. Trotting leisurely back to the treeline, she could more than hear the crashing through the forest, a low rumbling tremor that made her hackles rise.

She took off at once, the mission for food long abandoned, the instinct to return to her family overriding all. First she heard the unmistakeable whirring and grinding of machinery – huge beasts that devoured the earth and spat out human homes in its place. She didn't feel her legs tire.

Moving closer, she could hear the deep timbre of voices shouting and jeering. That, coupled with the harsh floodlights, was like a sensory overload, everything in her screaming at her to *get away!* But still she crept closer, flattening herself to the moist warm earth. There was a deep sense of wrongness in being so close; the smell; the sound; but she needed to know her sweet pups were okay.

The tracks left churned up mud in their wake, and she could see the small mound she had called home, where she had birthed and raised her young in – it was totally flattened, a shadow of what it once was. Letting out a keening cry, not dissimilar to the sound of a squalling new born child, she awaited a response. Something to let her know a miracle had happened, that her beautiful 12-day-old babies had survived the onslaught of the humans with their metal monsters.

Nothing.

Polly Micklewright, Housewife to two young children Shropshire.

The Turn

I thought she was playing with me. She had looked at me directly and smiled. But, as I reached out my paw to tickle her, she pulled her arm back and it changed, a bright red streak opening up along it. She screamed. I panicked and reached out again, this time slicing through her clothes and her chest. Now I didn't recognise her any more. She was red and glistening and...Tasty. Finally, I had caught my own dinner.

More running and screaming and, in the background, the head keeper points a long stick in my direction.

R.E. Stephens, Writer, Birmingham.

Letting the Elephant Out

She was watching me. She never moved, her gaze focused solely on where I sat. I looked back, wondering. I reached out to touch, my hand grasping her, the soft grey fur welcoming my palm. She continued to watch me. Emboldened, I picked her up, her body so tiny in my hands that she almost disappeared. Her ears were large, her eyes alight and her tusks a bright ivory. Her fur tickled my hands, a strange sensation that seemed to crawl around my fingers and up my arms, circling my elbows before rushing across the rest of my body. The world shrank to a pinpoint, the only image her face, before everything went black.

She was watching me from beyond the tree line, her eyes focused on the truck I was sat in. I felt as though she wasn't looking at the other people but was solely focused on me. Taking a deep breath, I opened the door, its hinges creaking as rust dropped onto the dusty ground. Around me, there were whispered warnings, hands reaching out to grab me, brushing off my shoulders as I ignored them and continued out of the truck.

Little clouds of dust formed under my feet as I landed on the soil, following me as I made my way across the open savannah. She never moved, her entire being watching me as I edged closer. I walked a little faster, never taking my eyes off of her. I became smaller and smaller, shrinking into the horizon as her stature loomed above me. I stopped when I was only a few feet away, holding my breath, waiting to see if she would charge. She never did; instead she simply watched me.

Up close I could see her eyes were deep and dark, holding the night sky within them, shrouded by curtains made to keep the rest of the world at bay. Her skin was leathery, lined with age, laugh lines stretching out from her eyes. That struck me as oddly human and as I continued to stare at her, I became more and more convinced that she understood us. Her trunk curled up and down at her feet, small hairs lining it, caught up in the evening savannah breeze. Nothing about her seemed threatening. Her feet, even though they were bigger than my head, appeared graceful, the half-moon shapes sunk into them, delicate and refined. Her ears remained tucked into her head but I knew if she had moved them, two replicas of Africa would sit on each side of her eyes. She was the embodiment of the savannah and as the sun began to set, she continued to look at me, and I at her, both caught up in the moment.

Then, with uninhabited grace, she turned her head, drawing my eyes behind her to the open savannah. Not too far away lay another elephant, almost an exact replica of the one in front of me, save for the aching space where its tusks should have been. Scarlet sand stained the ground around its head and human footprints scarred the area surrounding its body. The elephant in front of me turned her head again, squaring me with a pleading gaze, her eyes painfully human, and as we continued to stare at each other, the world around me descended into pounding black.

I sat back in my chair as the real world rushed back in pounding colour. I was still holding her in my hands, her soft fur still clasped in my palm. Quickly I put her back onto the desk next to me, trying to tell myself that I'd been dreaming. I turned back to my work but her eyes, riddled with unimaginable pain, and the evening heat from the savannah still lingered in my head.

Kathryn Cockrill, University Student/Author, UK.

It'll Ruin My Mercedes

"Have you seen these stupid scare tactics from the bloody environmental lobbyists?" Frank jabbed his finger so hard at the Special Edition Manly News, it went right through the paper. "Read this, 'In a matter of weeks, the sea-levels could rise to be level with The Corso.' "He peered out of his fourth-floor office window. "Apparently our nice street's gonna end up like Venice. And the car park? Well I suppose that'll be completely underwater. It'll ruin my Mercedes!" Frank laughed. "And what can we do?" he tipped his head back as he emptied the last glug of cappuccino into his mouth and tossed the cup in the green bin. "See, I'm doing my bit."

Konzi stroked Shelley the Labrador, enjoying her work environment whilst she still could. Ever since the first Tsunami hit the Australian coast the year before, people kept calling in sick saying that they couldn't bear to say goodbye to their furry friends every morning, for fear it might be the last. The 2025 Office Working Laws now allowed you to bring your pets to work.

Konzi turned toward her boss, considered keeping her mouth shut, but decided she didn't have anything to lose. "Recycling is all a bit last decade, Mr Kia."

"Please call me Frank." He nodded at her to continue; he didn't want to seem like he was a complete environmental moron.
"Frank. Now South Cap has gone, we're in the lap of the Gods." Her volume increased. "Only, not even the Gods can help us now. It's too late." Konzi held up one hand, angrily mocking the futile belief that an imaginary overseer would save everything that they'd messed up. "Recycling isn't going to make a difference anymore. Not here anyway." Furiously, she pointed in the direction of the ocean. "I'm only here because I want to be near one of the measurement zones, I want to see it with my own eyes. Australia is forefront in assessing the impact of the South Pole Ice Cap shift. My parents really want me to go to China to live with them inside the New Wall, but I can't just sit by." She stood up. "In Norfolk, they're digging a Super-Dyke to see if that saves them from the floods, so I'm going to England soon to help." She'd been trying to tell him for weeks.

"You are?" Frank turned sharply toward his newest junior exec. "I thought you were on my ten-year path to directorship?"

"Riiiiight." Konzi rolled her eyes as she slid past her boss toward the kitchen. "Mr Ki... I mean, Frank. Your business was one of the best performing in the early 20s. And this place used to be amazing, right between the harbour and the beach." She looked at him, "And so many great places to go for lunch." She mocked.

Frank glared at her, confused.

Konzi pointed outside, down at the groups of scientists who were expeditiously tapping on their tablets, huddled under huge sunshades at the temporary coffee-come-research spots.

"You do know we're in the hot zone here, don't you? The UN Climate committee said this is the last summer that this part of Australia will be liveable because of the floods and heat." She grabbed the newspaper off of Frank's desk. "Did you even read this?"

Frank waved it away. He'd been annoyed when the pub next door had turned into a cheap hostel and blamed that for all the hippy and academic types that lined the promenade when he went for his morning walks. "You young people, so negative. Perhaps the 'big iceberg' will get stuck at New Zealand. They've got lots of mountains so they can live up there instead."

"That 'big iceberg' used to be the bloody South Pole!" Konzi exclaimed, exasperated by Frank's ignorance.

"Well, it means we get to see more penguins in Manly." Frank grinned stupidly.

The previously, almost secret, population of Little Penguins had been practically wiped out by the much larger Emperors that had been relocated from the Antarctic in an attempt to save the species. None of them were faring well in the heat though.

Frank continued. "I like life here. We've always been at risk of skin cancer, so that's not changed. All this bloody cover-up every time you go outside business. It's too hot for long sleeves. And I wear sunscreen when I need to. Who knows what will happen tomorrow anyway? I might get hit by a bus!"

A year ago she might've wished that her backward-thinking-boss did get taken out by public transport, but his type would soon become extinct anyway from the massive radiation poisoning now occurring as a result of the lack of ice calming down the effects of the sun. Konzi sighed and pulled the office hand towels from the mini auto-washer under the sink.

"It'll be alright, Konzi. It's all gonna work out. They don't call me Frank Know-It-All for nothing."

Konzi slammed the laundry basket onto the floor, causing Shelly to bark. "You know K.I.A. also stands for Killed In Action!"

Frank was shocked. He'd never seen her so angry.

Konzi breathed out slowly and stroked Shelley. "I'm going onto the roof to hang out the washing. I assume you're Okay with me breaking those outdated by-laws that say we're not allowed to do that because it ruins the 'aesthetics'." She mocked his air quotes.

"Oh, that's good, that'll seem like we're really doing the environmental thing. Perhaps I should go buy a more environmentally-friendly car. I'm still using Petrol! I can't believe that a Mercedes is giving me a bad image! Perhaps I should get a boat instead. What is the world coming to?"

As Konzi opened the door, Shelley went berserk. The tidal wave warning alarm was going off. "It's already come."

Suzi Green, Consultant, Sydney.

LETTERS FROM THE CORRESPONDENCE PAGE OF *THE THYMES FOOD SUPPLEMENT*

1ˢᵗ May
To Whom It May Concern,

I read, with extreme consternation, a recent article in your supplement entitled *Veganism: A Moral Obligation.* In this piece, the writer states that since we know plants cannot feel physical pain and animals can, all people have a moral duty to eat plants rather than animals.

I take great umbrage with this notion. Humans decapitate us and rip us out of our beds all the time, whereas we plants have never done anything to them that merits such treatment. Unless you count carnivorous plants, but we never talk about them – the sadists.

Kindly reconsider and revise your views. You risk losing many of your green readers by allowing views such as these to be circulated in your publication.

Yours distressedly,
A Carrot.

8ᵗʰ May
Dear Carrot,

I am sorry that our article, *Veganism: A Moral Obligation* has caused you and other plants so much distress, necessitating the writing of the letter featured on last week's correspondence page. We were not aware that we had such a large number of green fans – this is very helpful for us to know.

Furthermore, you raise an interesting point about morality: what we do carries a moral implication, but whom we do it to can also imply moral judgement, and a sense of superiority.

We will certainly take your feedback into greater consideration when designing our content in the future. Meanwhile, thank you for taking the time to write to us.

Yours,
Hannah Rogers, chief editor of *The Thymes Food Supplement.*

15th May

Dear Carrot,

How *dare* you call us sadists? I'm an upstanding citizen who volunteers many hours of time giving pleasure to visitors at the Botanic Gardens in Glasgow, on an unpaid basis, to boot. It troubles me deeply that you and your kind have passed such hasty judgement on us, and then slandered us in a major food publication, to boot.

First of all, I cannot help being born with such sharp teeth, any more than you can help being born orange. Incidentally, don't you think that colour's a little loud and garish of you? I expect you know the rest of the plant community awkwardly averts their eyes when they catch sight of you being pulled up.

Secondly, the closure of my jaws upon being touched is a *reflex*. I am not some monster lying in wait for unsuspecting prey and then gleefully clamping down on them, affording them a slow and painful death. That's the stuff of humans who lay traps. Besides, small humans love it when I close on their fingers.

Thirdly, I can't help that live animals smell delicious. Can *you* help salivating and priming your photosynthesising chemicals when you see the first rays of sunlight spreading out over the rim of the hill? Ms Rogers, can *you* help salivating or your stomach rumbling if you're in a restaurant waiting to be served, and someone walks past you carrying a plate of your favourite food? Unlike *some* people, I don't pretend that all of what I like is morally all right, simply because it affords me pleasure.

I'm willing to consider forgiving you and the rest of the plant community, if you take a lesson from this incident and learn not to judge what you do not understand.

Yours outragedly,

A Venus Fly Trap.

22nd May

Dear Venus Fly Trap,

My apologies for the offence and upset caused to you, and to the other carnivorous plants in the Glasgow Botanic Gardens, by my thoughtless aside. Incidentally, colour shouldn't come into it either – I can't help being orange. That was a low hit.

It is clear to me now that there are no easy moral inferences when it comes to what we and others eat, how much control we have over our bodies, and how much suffering is caused. I am sorry I judged you and your kind so hastily.

Yours penitently,

A Carrot.

29th May

Dear Carrot,

I should not have brought colour into it. It was completely inappropriate and not relevant to the topic at hand, except as a bitter, childish retort on my part. Please accept my apologies.

Yours contritely,

Venus Fly Trap.

5th June

Dear Venus Fly Trap and Carrot,

I simply had to offer my contribution to this very thought-provoking and poignant discussion, which Ms Rogers has been so kind to publish week by week in its entirety. I, too, had never thought about the finer or less direct moral implications of veganism, as opposed to carnivorism or the use of animal products in a vegetarian capacity. I hope it will not cause you too much distress to learn that I and my kind are all strict herbivores. It pains me to say that I have eaten more than one carrot, though I have never yet eaten a venus fly trap. I mainly eat grass. Allow me to tell my story, for I have nothing to offer except for what has happened to me, as an animal kept by humans for their produce.

The field in which I live is about a quarter of a mile by a quarter of a mile. It slopes down towards a valley, and has a small river running through it. Normally I have no companions except for a tiny, fat, grey miniature Shetland called Bobbie. He doesn't speak the same language as me, but he and I enjoy grooming each other.

Last year, when the leaves on the Dutch Elm in the field next to mine began to turn golden and drop to the ground, a big thing pulled up at the structure from which the man comes to feed me each day. This structure was not red with large wheels, as the one that sometimes roars through my field is. Nor was it blue and fast-moving, with small wheels, like the one the man who feeds me sits on when he throws turnips at me. This one was dark blue, and had two parts to it – one part pulling the other. The part behind was made entirely of hard, grey material that gleamed in the light of the sun, and something big was stamping around inside it.

The man who feeds me opened a door in the grey, gleaming part of the thing, and out stepped the most beautiful creature that I have ever seen in my life. He looked like me, and yet not like me. His hair all over was shiningly clean and golden. The large, tight curls in which his hair fell on the area around his neck were exquisitely soft and delicate. He said nothing. He could easily have impaled the man who feeds me, with those sharp horns and the rippling muscles around his shoulders, but he walked quietly, and his large, brown eyes had a soft, kind look in them. Monty. I heard the man who feeds me call him that.

They left us together for one hour in a small, enclosed area beside my field shelter. As soon as the gate shut behind us he approached and sniffed me all over. I breathed deeply into his curls, enjoying the way they rippled like a ripe barley field in the wind. Feelings stirred within me, and we frisked around each other, both trying simultaneously to touch and smell as much of the other as possible with as much of ourselves as possible. When at last we came together I had the feeling of two halves becoming a whole. And then, as quickly as he had arrived, the man who feeds me opened the gate and led him away. I didn't know then what any of it meant. There was a curious, other-worldly feeling to it all – as if I'd been visited by an angel.

That winter was very different from the winter before, for several reasons. The man who feeds me didn't just deliver turnips and hay. I got barley feed, with something tangy added to it that I couldn't identify, but which I later came to crave at sudden, random times. My body felt heavier and my middle grew rounder, but not in an uncomfortable or painful way exactly, or in the way it does when I have eaten too fast, too much, or the wrong thing. Bobbie was as faithful a companion as ever, though I noticed he kept a respectful distance. By the time the snow fell, I was experiencing sensations I had never felt before – as though my insides, and the food passing through them, were alive and moving within me. At first I dismissed these as unusual tummy rumblings, but when a sharp something jabbed outwards from the inside, I realised that something entirely new was going on, though what it was I couldn't imagine.

The mushy, muddy ground of the field next to mine hardened, then softened, then dried a little and yielded its first fresh shoots, as the river thawed and new leaves began to appear in clusters on the Dutch Elm. Some birds crawled, honking, across the sky in V-shapes. Some chirped sharply in the roof of my field shelter, fluttering back and forth between the rafters. Others called across the valley, their voices rising to a pitch and then trilling on the wind. Once the field next door had a good crop of grass I would be turned out into it – the field I had wintered in was getting rather bare even before the snow set in.

One day, as the moon shone white in the clear morning sky, my middle squeezed in a mildly painful way, without my telling it to do so. It was as if a drawstring muscle across it that I hadn't been aware of before, had been pulled tight. I tried to explore with a hoof, but by now my middle had grown so round that I couldn't get my leg up far enough to kick away anything that might have been grabbing at me. The sensation repeated itself, and the pain, this time, was sharper. The tightness and pain came at more frequent intervals, and grew more intense, until each one made me bellow. The man who feeds me came out and ran his hand over me. He nodded, said "Easy, girl. Gently, now," and guided me into my field shelter. The light inside shone yellow, and fresh straw had been laid on the ground.

The next pain caused my front legs to buckle, and I rolled onto my side. Terrified that I might not be able to get up again, I struggled, but my legs merely flailed. The man said some other words that I didn't understand, in a low voice. When I'm not well he gets help or does something, so I knew then that I wasn't unwell, and instead focussed on another new feeling under my tail. A feeling of being stretched, wider and wider until it hurt, and then wider still until the pain was all-consuming, but I couldn't stop the bearing down that was causing whatever it was to stretch me and turn me inside out. Plants reading this will not be able to understand the sensation. And all this time, the rhythmic, fiery tightening kept pulsing through my belly.

53

Suddenly there was a wet rush, and whatever had been making my middle so heavy and round all winter – whatever alien had been kicking and shifting within all these months – came free, and sloshed out onto the ground behind me. The rhythmic tightening dropped away to sporadic twinges. The stretching stopped. I could move again, struggled to my feet, and turned to look. There, in a mess of discharge and blood, was a tiny, wet, new cow. Who knew tiny cows could swim and grow in bigger cows?

From where had she come? She had Monty's curls and my ears. Somehow my body had taken something from this angelic golden being, and something from deep within me, and made an entirely new someone with a little of both of us mixed in, and who, I now realised, was at this point in time, completely dependent upon me to keep her alive.

That was when the man who feeds me and cares for me, who protects me from harm and who reassures me, put a towel over her so I couldn't finish licking her, picked her up and carried her away. I don't know where she went. I never saw her again. Maybe she's with Monty now. After my body had rid itself of one more shapeless, blooded mass, the man cleaned out my field shelter so that I didn't even have the scent of her anymore. But he couldn't erase the fact that she had been here, or that I was meant to be with her. After the sun had set and risen one more time, yet another uncomfortable, full sensation started in the sensitive, hanging, hairless part towards the back of my underbelly. The man who feeds me washed me there, and then pushed and pulled certain parts in certain ways which caused something to whoosh out in spurts. I knew this was meant for the little one. I hoped it would get to her somehow. When he had finished, I felt less full and uncomfortable.

Monty has come to me many more times since then, and the whole process has repeated itself in a yearly cycle. I don't know where those little ones we made together have gone – there must be a whole herd of them somewhere. My soul is fragmented, and parts of it are missing. I would like to reunite with them someday and see who they have grown into, though I'm not now naïve enough to believe I ever will.

I have shared this account with you because it is all I have to offer personally about the use of animal products. I'm not trying to shame those who use them – merely to offer an alternative perspective through providing insight into what it's been like for me. Whatever you feel, I hold no resentment and harbour no bitterness. Bitterness will not be what brings my little ones back. I wish you all the very best.

Yours always,

A Cow.

12th June

Dear Cow,

What a story. Thank you so much for sharing it with us. I'm so sorry you've been through this trauma, and continue to go through it. It is a terrible thing to lose a child. I am forced to witness the annual decapitation of thousands of my own kind every year when you and your kind are turned out into my field, and I cannot even run away from it all as it happens.

That is not me trying to make you feel guilty either – you, too, have to eat. If only there were some way whereby none of us had to prey on each other for survival! In current absence of that way, I simply acknowledge you as a fellow being, and wish you peace and all good things in this world in which we all live.

Yours sympathetically,

A Common Grass Species.

14th September

Dear Professor Fawkes,

We at *The Thymes Food Supplement* have read, with great excitement and interest, your papers proposing a procedure for the genetic modification of animals, to implant chlorophyll into their fur and hair. This is a tremendously exciting notion – sunlight for energy for all! No more predators, no more prey. We recognise that there are complex ethical issues involved in any research, and that this breakthrough is still some years away and will be controversial once available. Nevertheless, we wish to extend a word of support towards you and your team, and express an interest in promoting this procedure when it becomes available.

Meanwhile, if there is anything we can do to speed this research along or contribute to its funding, please do not hesitate to let us know.

Yours in hope,

A Carrot; a Venus Fly Trap; a Cow; a Common Grass Species; and Hannah Rogers, chief editor of *The Thymes Food Supplement.*

Laura Guthrie, Writer, Inverness-Shire.

In the Moment

I sighed as I put down my pack and straightened my spine. Not quite two days into a five-day walk through the wilds of South West Tasmania and already my pack felt twice as heavy as when we started. I looked down at my seated companion. She smiled at me. She was fitter than me and a much more experienced bush walker. I wanted to conceal my discomfort from her for as long as possible.

'How you going?' she asked. 'Everything OK?'

'Yes,' I lied, 'but I'll be pleased to put the pack down for the day.'

'Not much further now. This will be our last stop before we camp. It's a bit early to stop for the day.' She looked at the sky. 'Sun will be going down soon, but we will get there in the light – just.'

I smiled back and bent to pull out my water bottle as she sought out a snack from the top of her pack.

I straitened up again as I prepared to drink, and movement at the top of the little rocky escarpment in front of me drew my attention. An animal was squeezing through the dense bushes and coming into the open. A feral dog. Medium size but with a rather long snout. Not the sort of place I would have expected to see one.

I saw it, and it saw me. As soon as it did, it turned and scuttled back into the bushes, but as it turned, it exposed its flank. Its striped flank!

'TIGER!' I shouted and started to race towards the rocks.

'What? ... Oh!' called my companion, and I heard her start after me.

She reached the top of the rocks just seconds after I did. Without speaking, we both knew there was no hope of pursuing the mysterious beast, through the tiny tunnel in the undergrowth. The rocks where it had stood were hard, dry and bare – nothing to hold a footprint. No evidence but from my eyes.

'How sure are you?'

'Pretty sure. It didn't occur to me it was anything but a dog until it turned and I saw its stripes.'

'There are a few striped breeds of dogs, you know.'

'Yes, but this one only had stripes towards its back legs, and only coming part way down its sides. It really looked just like the pictures.'

'Then you are a *very* lucky man!' She smiled and kissed my cheek.

We climbed back down and hurried to our camp spot in the remaining light.

At the end of the walk, I reported my sighting of course. Only one viewer, no photo, no additional evidence. Not really very convincing proof for the scientific community.

But I saw the animal and in the moment that it turned sideways to me, I knew that the thylacine lives.

Geoff Covey, Semi-retired Chemical Engineer, Brisbane.

Dark Waters

Wasn't the world such a beautiful place?

Once the sky was crystal blue, the air so clean, the fragrance of trees and blossoms lingered in the air like invisible fairies. Once the grass was emerald green, daisies and buttercups growing in rows, dancing in the clear breeze. Once the day was so beautiful, the golden sunshine would cast a radiant glow upon the earth, making the ocean look almost crystalized.

I used to swim across that ocean, gliding merrily across the waves as the sun shone brightly in the cloudless sky. I would join my pod as we swam together in perfect unison, believing no one or anything could harm us.

But all that changed.

Toxic chemicals now float in the air, combing themselves with water droplets, making acid rain. Industrial waste and oil are thrown into the sea, the air unclean and dirty. There is a taste that I do not recognise; it tastes and feels bad. It makes my eyes sting and my fellow dolphins find it so unbearable as we try to keep together to find at least one last spot that is clean.

Once the water was sparkly blue, but now it is a midnight black and yet I know it's not merely us beneath the waves that suffer; I see seagulls flapping above us, desperately trying to fly but with great difficulty as sticky substances cling to their wings. Fish float above the surface, their frail bodies no longer capable of taking in the toxic waters, whilst the foul odour in the air takes over the previous smell of seaweed and salt.

And still these people's eyes gaze upon us with great delight, despite being partially to blame for why our lives are like this now. They show no remorse for their environmental crimes. They simply stare at us, admire us, and mock us before bringing more damage to our home.

The rain once represented purity and cleanliness, but now the acidic drops mix in with the seawater, making it more harmful than before. Is this how low humanity has sunk? Will there be no rest to this wickedness? My family is dying out, slowing, and there is nothing I can do to stop it.

I wish that I could tell them my story. But they will never hear me.

Lauren Johnson, Social Media Volunteer, West Midlands.

Elephants Never Forget

I remember when I had a mother. Those days are hazy now, but they grow clearer at night. I remember how she wrapped her strong trunk around me, lifting me when I stumbled, calming me when I fell. Telling me I would learn. That life was good. That everything would be okay.

In my dreams, I still see her curled up beside me. I hear her breathing and the peaceful drone of crickets. I remember how much she loved me. But then I wake and see the thick chains around my ankles and feel the dull ache in my back, the weeping sores on my feet.

I remember the day she was killed. The shot that broke the air. The dull thud as she fell to the ground. The tears as I cried. I try to forget, but elephants never forget. I remember the men, the shouts and the torturous pain as they forced me to leave. In my head, I hear my screams and feel the hook reaching, deep, deep into my soul. How I yearn to see my family again, but instead I'm alone with my mahout until the sun appears above the plains and the people arrive. Small ones, tall ones, overweight, goofy ones. People with their clunky cameras, gleaming white grins and noise. People smelling of sweat, spice and urine. They smack my flanks and yank at my trunk.

'See how he smiles,' they say. 'What a cute elephant.'

As I gaze into the lens, I feel the firm hand of the mahout on my back. He's quiet now. Almost kind. Answering their questions in a sweet, gentle voice, while he strokes my ears and tells them of our bond.

'Aah,' they say. 'Ooh.'

Today, a middle-aged couple squeeze their hefty bulk into my howdah.
'What a tight fit,' says the lady and laughs. My heart is heavy but my head is light, and while I trudge up the hill, the world begins to spin. And as it spins, I spot my mother. Just for a second. A brief, flickering second. And when I do, I raise my trunk to the sky.

'Harumph, Harumph,' I trumpet.

And for a moment, the blue seems bluer and the sun seems brighter. But then, she is gone.

'Please come back,' I plead. 'Please.' I sink onto my knees and lower my head to the earth, ignoring the cries of the people and the crazy yells of the mahout. The anger will come later. But for now, I don't care.

'He's never done this before, ma'am. I don't know what's come over him.'

'We will sue, you know. That's what happens in our country.'

I close my eyes. Try in vain to see her again, but all I can hear is the gun. The thud. All I can feel are the chains, the sores and the throbbing pain as the mahout begins to whack my back.

Mary Thompson, Freelance teacher/tutor, UK.

Autumn Ceremony

Low-slanting, mellow sunglow warmed the grey walls of the ruined tower. It was the feast of Mabon, the Autumn Equinox, when days and nights are of equal length. Open to the sky, the tower sheltered thirteen gathered in a silent circle. Crowned with red-gold leaves, the priestess stood apart as the others watched with avid concentration. She stood with her arms outstretched, facing north, where a small table was laden with windfall apples, yellow grain and a few late roses. In her right hand was a small, iron knife with a dark wood handle. Facing the altar, she drew the first of four cardinal pentagrams with the blade. The ceremony had begun.

Outside the wall, invisible to the celebrants, the air rippled as though with heat and a wavering figure appeared. The face, with its grass-green, up-slanted eyes, was unforgettable. It looked tired and drawn, criss-crossed with the tiny lines of an unbearable sorrow. A pair of pale, curved horns rose from lank grey hair. The bare torso was painfully thin, the skin stretched tightly over the ribs. Below the waist, mangy grey haunches curved into bony hoofs. Near him on the ground lay three dead things: the remains of a Michaelmas daisy, shriveled black by weed-killer, a bee and a woodpecker, its bright feathers ruffled and soiled.

Inside the tower, people held hands as the ritual moved to a circle dance. Slowly, gently at first, then at a more vigorous pace, they coiled in and out, again and again. The chain of dancers whirled with sinuous strength, beating the earth with their feet until the ground seemed to rock. As they reached the center once more, the priestess commanded them to stop. Hot with exertion, they sat in silence around a leaf-covered, wooden platter, stilled their minds and waited. When the priestess revealed its contents, they gazed in silence at the tiny offering: a solitary ear of corn, emblem of the harvest, a time of ripeness and balance between the seasons. Transforming the energy generated by the dance, each celebrant melted their individual consciousness into a communal state of trance, breathing deeply in the fragrant afternoon air. The theme of their meditation was seasonal bounty, harmony with nature and respect for all forms of life. As the meditation intensified, the hybrid entity outside began to change. His flesh grew plump and rosy, the lines etched on his forehead softened and his fur became sleek again.

The ceremony reached its height. As the celebrants rose, a wooden goblet filled with cider and a plate of ripe hazelnuts were served to each person in turn. The watcher's eyes lit up and his lips curved into a smile. Raising a pipe of reeds to his mouth, he started to blow, softly at first, then a wild, fierce melody flowed out, then faded into the glowing air. Near his hoofs, now hardly more than a pattern in the fallen leaves, a gradual stir of movement began. The blackened petals of the Michaelmas daisy grew purple once more. The bee buzzed and the woodpecker spread its glorious wings and soared away into the trees. When people emerged, awed at the music's rapture and speaking very softly, there was no one visible against the sinking sun.

Anna Powell, Retired lecturer and scholar, Anglesey.

Breathe

I talk, but you don't listen. I could see, but you have taken my eyes. I feel, but you don't want to believe that I can. For all of these years I have offered you shelter, food, the air that you breathe. I've given life, my plants have healed and my branches have provided shelter for the young. I've given you beauty, so much beauty. My leaves were the brightest of greens, they floated in the air shrouded in cloud. When I rained, I gave you all of my water and when I stopped, my sun shone the brightest, and colours mixed in the sky. My birds sang the oldest of songs, tuned to perfection millenia ago, and my insects moved excitedly keeping my world alive, spreading their colours and patterns throughout the forest. The cats and the monkeys ruled throughout and were quick and breathtaking to behold. I bloomed in the brightest of colours and most intoxicating smells. I made you feel free, I made you feel whole, and I made you realise that you are home when you are with me.

We worked together at first, you humans used your hands and learnt my ways. You discovered my mysteries, you respected me and I gave you my secrets so you could use them to your advantage. I could be harsh and cruel, it's a challenge to survive with me, but I gave you life, real life, a life of freedom and peace to be one with the earth that you came from.

Then the greed came, and people forgot that they and I are bound together by nature. My roots were torn up by the mile and I screamed in agony, but you wouldn't listen. My babies died, the insects, animals and trees that were a part of me were burnt, trashed, and removed. Each time I gave all I could to grow your crops, to tend to your cattle, but it was never enough. Each time my soils were sucked dry of nutrients, you didn't care and you found a fresh patch of me to suck clean. You violated me down to my core, ripping my minerals from deep within me, claiming them for your own at my expense. And still, it wasn't enough, no matter how much I gave, there was no reprieve.

I saw some of you humans try to protect me, to learn about me, to help one another take care of me, but there were always so many more people with so many more weapons to tear me apart. I ached, my torso stripped bare, and I was left rotting as nothing could stop

65

this destruction. As I lay dying, I breathed out my last oxidised breathes. I didn't have the strength to suck in all the carbon that you needed me too, I didn't have the energy to wrap the carbon dioxide into my roots, my trunks, my leaves. I didn't have the will to keep giving to those who only take. As I lay crippled and sore, my beauty withered and my life languishing, I watched you panic. You panicked as my pain turned to anger and became treacherous thunderstorms which drowned the Earth, as my fury scorched hot land hotter and froze cold lands colder. I tried to pity you as you found all your homes to be uninhabitable and existence became painful, but I could not. I had given you everything, all of my life, and as the waters rose around you and your homes were lost, I hoped you were thinking of all the life that you extinguished in me.

I saw people crying, they came to stand under the last of my shade and feel the last of my life, realising with overwhelming fear that here was something that couldn't be fixed with their money. Your greed is empty, your realisations come too late, and you cannot buy my health.

As I fade away into the darkness, I look forward to the day your species will join me in obsoletion. I hope that those other species who have survived will revive themselves in their numbers, evolve, diversify, respect whatever is left of me in a way that humans never could, or would. The Earth will keep going, humans have slain themselves, but I must breathe my last breath, and cry my last tear. Goodnight.

Stephanie Martin, Tropical Forest Ecology Masters Student, and Science Communicator, UK.

Deathly Premonitions - The hunt for the black rhino

One of the many things that I love about Zimbabwe are the names that people, birds and animals are given, the simplistic way in which they receive a name that describes them. On the hunt for the black rhino, I met the 'Go Away' bird, so called because of its nasal cry of "g'way" and, as the Zimbabwean rangers told me, its ability to utter a plaintive call from high up above at inopportune moments, giving away a person's position and causing them to whisper angrily "Go away!"

However, this story is not about the birds of this beautiful country but about the elusive black rhino, and how we tracked and nearly found it.

Today, we arrive at a remote outpost situated on a headland overlooking the vast and beautiful Lake Kariba. Traveling in traditional African style, we have rumbled over many miles of dusty tracks flanked by thorny acacia bushes, jolted and bumped about on unkempt roads, perched precariously on the roof top of a landrover. Albeit a rather uncomfortable mode of travel, this has afforded us fantastic views of a wealth of wildlife - elephants, loitering in low scrub land, each with their own personal white Ibis, waterbuck springing across to the safer side of river banks and a herd of bush pigs foraging in amongst the roots of a baobab tree.

The watery inlets either side of the outpost provide Vietnamese and Chinese poachers with an "off the beaten track" route into black rhino territory. It is here that the rangers who dedicate their lives to protecting black rhino live and operate from. Based in a rather shabby looking wooden hut, they have a frugal lifestyle yet show us the usual abundance of Zimbabwean charm and warmth. The British government have given some funding to the anti-poaching project and we are visiting to see how the money is being spent and to meet the rangers. Of course, we would also love to catch of glimpse of the black rhino whilst we are here. This fantastic beast, who is not black at all but is called so due to the black mud that it rolls in and to distinguish it from the more prevalent white rhino, is a shy, solitary character unaware of the great lengths that the conservationists here are going to, to prevent its extinction.

After the customary chat and offer of rooibos tea, we stretch our legs and have a look at Kariba - a flooded valley and drowned forest under which lies a village. The lake provides hydro-electric power to Zambia and Zimbabwe and is ocean like in proportions. In August, the dry season is nearly at an end and many birds and animals are drawn to the shores to drink. The air is filled with an orchestral amount of noise – the sea eagle providing the shrill and mournful strings section, baboons the vocal acrobatics of the tune, and the sonorous baritone grunts of the hippo being the percussion. There is, needless to say, no sign at all of a rhino.

The rangers suggest we take a more proactive approach and look for evidence of rhino activity in the nearby scrub, then maybe try to track one. But first, there are rules - the black rhino likes to browse in the grasslands and koppies around Kariba but is a reticent and wary. Being almost blind, what a rhino lacks in visual awareness is more than made up for in finely attuned hearing and, unlike his white rhino cousin, the black rhino will run "through" danger as opposed to "round it". This clearly adds some peril to the tracking activity and, as such, requires the ranger to carry a gun. There are more rules - due to the black rhino's excellent auditory skills, we must walk as silently as possible in order not to alert him and he has an admirable sense of smell so perfume and aftershave must be removed. That said, we are ready to find him and within a short distance of the outpost, evidence starts to emerge that he may have been nearby recently.

The ranger, silently very excited, points to some tracks in the dust. They are indeed the prints of a black rhino and we establish the direction that he, or she, may be travelling in. We set off in single file following the footprints, making every attempt to breathe quietly, stepping with exaggerated caution to avoid noisy twigs and, even when the occasional acacia thorn abrades us, we merely mouth pain to avoid disturbing our target.

Sometime later, we are becoming more aware of the intensity of the sun, the bushes we are walking through are no more than midriff in height and there is no shade to be had. The heat is becoming uncomfortable and sweat is breaking out on my face and back, when suddenly the ranger alerts us to more evidence of rhino activity – spoor or droppings, and fresh ones too! He eagerly mimes that the freshness of the dung tells him that we are gaining on the rhino and that we may encounter our elusive creature over the next rise or around the next corner. Heads lowered, we carry on and our anticipation builds as we notice that the leaves of the black rhino's favourite bushes have been nibbled delicately in true rhino fashion with the prehensile hooked lip that is characteristic of the species. Surely our meeting is imminent. Each clamber over Zimbabwe's trademark rocky outcrops sees gazelles take flight, each rounding of a bend disturbs a warthog feeding but nothing more than that. Every snap of a branch or crunch underfoot causes us to stand stock still then carefully reach for our cameras. Our ranger goes on ahead, his face animated, promising that he will locate our black rhino and return to collect us. He arrives back, crestfallen.

The sun has moved positions in the sky; we have walked in silence and followed the trail for some miles yet the black rhino continues to evade us. We feel that maybe there is a twinkle in his weakly sighted eyes as he moves just ahead of us, tantalisingly close, but undetected. I am willing us to find him and I look ahead through a haze of dust, wondering if I can just make out that iconic silhouette in the shimmering heat, or whether my mind is playing tricks on me and it is merely an illusion. As the scorching breeze blows sand and dust to cover the tracks and the spiny shrubs seem strangely untouched, I hope that our trail has not become a deathly premonition.

* * *

For some years around 2007, numbers of black rhino were becoming dangerously low. Organised gangs of poachers, driven by the demands of the Asian market, were systematically slaughtering these endangered creatures despite Zimbabwe's efforts to protect them in their Lowveld regions. Being a rhino in possession of not one but two horns, the black rhino was of particular interest to certain countries within the Far East who had a particular penchant for rhino horn as a medicine.

Susanne Allcroft, Secondary School Teacher, North Wales.

Eel Odyssey

Her wide-mouthed grin rises from the murk, siren-singing soon-to-be sojourner on the seas, top predator in the pond at home, her feral-spotted scales silvered in moonlight. Flirty-finned and lithe as Esther Williams in the pool, not so *dangerous when wet*, she's a 20-million-egg mermaid mooching after ducklings, crunching young carp with plate-like teeth.

But change is coming, a ripening: at autumn's rainy imperative she'll up stakes, undulate from park or edgy dam, swimcrawlslide from fresh to brackish to salt, slither through wetland and golf-course by night, fin-over-fin through corridors of swamp and sedge-grass, down past the third runway to pour the dark wine of her body into Botany Bay.

Up there in the Coral Sea she's a voyager horizontal-nosing in the depths by day, vertical as an exclamation mark by night. Gut and anus dissolved – no more eating – her body's silver now, lured by moon and tides or some ancestral Pangaean memory to spawn in warmer waters where she began. Exhausted, she'll die there in new-moon days, drift to the bottom of a deep dark sea.

Return of the elvers*: larvae travel incognito, curled leaves on the current. Then, glass eels flitting through seas with haunted eyes, thin arrows of spine. Sluiced by currents, piloted by magnetic fields into harbours, homing into river-mouths they've never known, or else minced in turbines, trapped in the fyke-nets of sushi traffickers.

Still, wave after wave of survivors launch tail-first over weirs and slipways, acrobats slithering through storm-drains, elvers rising, flinging themselves at inland dams soft-furred with moss. Ancient brains hard-wired for night-heat and motion, cued for the smell of mud and pond, sinuous s-bends unwinding from grass to wetness and trailing weed.

The miracle and mystery of eels, alive with the urgency of being alive, the iron will to arrive.

Louise Wakeling, Teacher & Writer, Australia.

Forager

I'll have to go further today, foraging for breakfast. The house has been bulldozed, the land around it dug up, everything flattened. They'll be erecting a larger building, high and wide, a human hive. The noise!

They have felled the ash that, from her girth, had stood for one hundred years or more, wonderful for shade, her wind-whispers an invitation to all. The garden is gone: the lovely garden with its roses and lavender, its generous buddleia that had self-seeded in the path to the pond, the green pond with its ballet of damselflies. You could catch the scent a long way off.

The old woman who lived there - died or taken away - sat in the sun, sipping chamomile tea. Chamomile! In my memory, I search and find the scent of it. She would watch me at my plundering and smile: "Is it you, honeybee, come back for more? Feel free!" She was the only one who ever made me welcome.

Jan McCarthy, Writer, Birmingham.

The Border Gate

There is a steep climb to the start of the walk, and the path skirts the edge of a hill fort towards the ridge. I notice first the wind; the rain stings but is not wet. The ordinary becomes extraordinary if you look for it and so I do. Short spikey grasses hold low down brightness of yellow pollen and a chaos of gorse spreads flowerful heady incense of coconut edged in vanilla across the landscape. As we climb, the vista reveals itself as round hills in a stretched landscape. But the mizzle is all around, cloud below cloud, in all the tones of grey. The two paths divide at the fingerpost and we press on towards the stone dyke that marks the line between Scotland and England. The Border Gate.

There are sheep with lambs on the hills, graffitied in matching blue spots. We stop by a low col between two rises, hunker down behind the wall and share coffee from a flask.

Lindy first found the newborn, and thinking it had come through the fence, lifted it and put it back where it had not come from. By the time I reached the fence, I saw a shivering, scrunched in a straggly patch of heather; no other sheep anywhere in sight. I was on my own in action and sentiment. I pushed passed and shrugged off not-so-helpful hands and silent needle glares, struggled to open the gate into the adjoining field and walked closer to the creature. The wind was so strong and loud it blanketed the harsh comments; the leave-it-alone commands. I caught her easily as she was so weak and light, all bone and no fluff but with sharp eyes and a fine speckled brow of white and black. Her fleece stained green with meconium was still in tight curls, which no ewe had licked warm or dry. I wrapped her in a plastic bag and she took some water from my hand, but I had no plans, no experience, no logic.

My one, probably irrational decision, to interfere with sheep on hills, farming methods, natural selection and ethics generally, suddenly left my relationship with the others in an impossible state of psychological tension. An argument with no words and fierce emotional territory to traverse: acute agitation fixed in blue staring. It is a difficult thing to describe how a feeble lamb can have such a catastrophic effect on human relationships, but a border had been crossed. I am suddenly a protector, not well versed in animal rescue, and I cannot let go. The lamb nuzzles.

We stupidly all walk on the way we intended, into increasing wind and driving rain, decision-less. I am caught by my own temerity and I leave others to work on the logistics.

'You *have* to leave the lamb, here by this rock; sheltered....'

The words are empty orders. The animal in my arms would not last an hour, exposed in this wind. I would rather it died in my arms.

At the bottom of the steep slope, in rapidly worsening weather, we discuss again, although I am hardly taking part; even without a lamb, we would not make The Schill. We turn around with the lamb in her bag in my arms and climb back up the long, steep hill we have just climbed down. I feel nothing of the weight in my arms but am terrified of the gulf I have opened in the group.

It's not about those who care and those who don't. I made a mistake and now in punishment, my physical capability is also challenged. The lamb is to be passed to the youngest member of the group.

'You might fall'.

Unable to protest, my precious lamb is snatched from me and dumped into anxious arms. Our group of five, town bred women, with an average age of sixty-four, trudging along narrow sheep tracks in worsening conditions, makes a comic sketch out of life and death.

The judgement call was made against me: I was not allowed to summon any counter argument. But at least there is no subterfuge, no double-crossing, no secret plan to abandon the lamb while my back is turned. I feel bereft and responsible because the lamb has the scent of many human hands by now and no ewe will re-accept it.

Returned to the car, two of us are dispatched with the still wrapped lamb to find the farm. Lindy drives slowly up to Halterburn Head, past bedraggled blanketed horses, passed old dumped washing machines and abandoned fridge-freezers, past skinny sheep in dirty pens and into the farmyard. A filthy door is open and the television is on, showing a blue screen through the dark window. I feel uneasy.

'Hello, hello,' I call. But no one comes.

Music plays loudly in an open barn. We step in and out beyond, through an opposite unlocked door, into another untidy courtyard. There are new supplies of baled sawdust stacked awkwardly and a metal horse exercising walk-about revolves silently, minus the horse.

A figure approaches; young and unkempt. A farmer watching television in the middle of the afternoon? I apologise if we are trespassing.

'We found a lamb on the hilltop and didn't know what to do,' I stutter.

I am nervous, but the fate of the lamb is no longer mine to influence. He removes her from the warm plastic bag and dangles her expertly by the front feet so that the belly and the umbilical cord are exposed.

'Not more than twenty-four hours old. You say you found her on Whitelaw Nick?'

He tips his forehead towards the hill behind us. His tone gives nothing away. I am not at all confident of a positive outcome. I notice that his overalls are stained and the pocket torn. A man of few words, he turns and walks away with the hanging, bleating lamb in his left hand, the plastic bag empty on the ground where he dropped it.

'I hope we did right?' I say.

Barbara Claridge, Wild Writing, Literature and Landscape MA at the University of Essex, Head Teacher, Brittany.

Succinction

My son Alistair once told me that an upside to the sixth mass extinction would be the loss of all those long Latin names for animals I and other naturalists delighted in.

"Succinctly extinct," he said, between mouthfuls of bacon. "Succinction."

"Sextinction," his sister Joanna chimed in. They both snorted.

"You wait!" I waggled a finger at them. "You wait until the food chain collapses."

They did not wait. Like most young people, they packed off to the cities long ago, where at least some semblance of civic order remained.

They both wrote to me, Joanna more than Alistair. In her last email, she said the floodwaters had reached just below her second floor flat. "You should come here. You want to see wading birds, you only need throw open your windows."

A week later, the Internet flickered its last. By the God who has deserted us, I am glad they are not here to see what has become of me and the sanctuary.

***

Visitors once thronged this hide, consulting their books and fiddling with binoculars. Even now, I fight the impulse to peer through the slits. This used to be a great spot for spoonbills. How I miss them, those ungainly waders, trailing their paddles of beaks through the water like tired cleaners, dragging heavy vacuums.

My son was wrong about my attachment to Latin names. I much prefer the pithy Anglo- Saxon ones. "Smew" – it should have been the word for a bodily noise, somewhere between a wheeze and a squeak of a fart.

All I've seen this year are swallows, darting above the marsh.

I used to think it was the extinction of the great beasts that would really hurt: whales, lions, elephants. That, at least, was a pain I anticipated. What I didn't foresee was the ache of extinct language. I don't mean the languages that disappeared with the people who spoke them, although that, of course, was a tragedy in itself. No, I mean chunks of language that lurk in our minds, like the smashed remnants of a wreck in the water. They float, displaying their barnacled rotting sides, taunting us with visions of a way of life only recently snatched from our grasp.

"What are you going to do with your life?" my mother once asked me. (Ornithology was not the answer she wanted. *No son of mine will turn into a professional bird watcher.*)

Nobody asks anyone else what they intend to do with their life any longer. It was a question I could not bring myself to ask my own precious children once they reached adolescence. We no longer 'do'. We are done to – by the floods, the droughts, the storms, and, worse of all, by each other.

It's not so much the defunct phrases that hurt, as those that linger on our tongues despite the demise of what they describe. Plans, whatever plans we can make, still 'come to fruition', despite the withering of almost every species of fruit tree you can think of. Those that were not done for by the passing of bees were blasted by the droughts.

I suppose that's why the visits from my neighbours have become ever greater in frequency and terser in tone.

When they first moved in, they were friendly: three brothers hoping to salvage what they could of their father's farm. A fine farm it was too: fallow fields and healthy herds of livestock. I watched the cows dwindle, year upon year. You can see the rib cages of the remaining beasts, like broken xylophones, flies buzzing round their gummy eyes. I doubt the brothers get much milk from them. Or meat, when they resort to slaughter.

No surprise, then, that they turned to hunting.

They were apologetic when they first turned up at the sanctuary, rifles smacking against their thighs.

"You'll get a hefty chunk of the profit, once it comes in." "It's only until our harvests improve."

Such a tenuous, precious thing, human optimism. Like a strand of a spider's web weighed down by dew, it bows so deep, until you swear it will break.

I agreed, of course. We all participated in the polite fantasy that I had a choice and was not intimidated in any way by their weapons. They promised me they would not shoot the rarer wading birds, just the common mallards and geese. 'Common' is not as common as it used to be.

***

At least the late summer light retains its amniotic, golden beauty. There is some comfort to be had there. A rustle in the shrubbery near the marsh makes me sit up. I fumble with my binoculars, hot fear prickling over my scalp. I see the muzzle of a gun between branches.

Resignation battles in my mind with a curdled anger and hatred.

I know they are only trying to keep themselves alive. But must we play this heedless violence out to the end?

I stumble out of the hide.

I must be quite a sight now, unshaven in ripped old clothes. A madman.

One of them shouts something I can't quite make out. A threat? Very good.

I spread my arms out like a scarecrow. "Go on then," I croak. "Get it over and done with. I'll make a better meal than any scrawny bird you take a shot at."

One of the brothers emerges, his thinning hair covered in twigs and dead leaves.

He points his gun upwards, barely a glance to spare for little ole me.

I turn around, just in time to see a vivid scuff of blue against the grey of the sky. It is the unmistakable iridescence of a kingfisher, the first I've seen in many a year.

A shot echoes out across the estuary, just before my shriek.

The bird's crumpled form against the sky is like a hastily dashed apostrophe: head down, wings to the fore. A word hanging in expectation of its final, silent syllable.

Anna Orridge, English as a Foreign Language Teacher, UK

19 Chestnut Road

Shade dappled the ground like sparks and the parched summer grass was just beginning to show signs of life from the early Autumn rain. The small scattering of leaves made a lazy attempt to flutter in the half-hearted breeze. Occasionally, sunlight would catch on the berries in the hedge and a spectrum of reds, oranges and purples would be revealed. The garden, although never completely silent, was resting.

The house had been empty for several years before the Parson family moved in. The small bungalow, amid a large wilderness, was the perfect plot for a project. It wouldn't be long before it suffered the same fate as the others that used to mirror it along the road. Small dwellings built in the 1950's for small families. Large gardens, part of the old country estate, were crowned with a beautiful array of trees. Mighty oaks and horse chestnuts stood guard over the smaller silver birch, hazel and holly. A utopia where flora, fauna and families could reside in harmony.

Decades later and things were different. Bungalows had given way to large, square five-bedroomed homes. Trees were lost to developments and gardens had shrunk. The Parson's plot, the last of its kind on the road, was soon to follow suit. Mr Parson had decided that clearing the garden was the first step to creating his perfect home. Planning had already been granted to remove the two silver birches that towered over the house, on the condition that they were replaced with something similar. In all good faith, a pair of tiny saplings had been purchased and were in buckets awaiting planting right at the bottom of the garden.

Whilst the children were armed with rakes and buckets to collect leaves, Mr Parson fired up the petrol strimmer. As it coughed into life, the loud stutter startled the pigeons in the tree above. Flapping wildly, they took off into the sky. This was shortly followed by a squirrel emerging from its drey, inquisitive to this intriguing new noise. The children laughed as they watched it scamper to the end of the branch, lean over and tilt its head in interest. Even Mr Parson had to smile at the puzzled expression on the little rodent's face. As he revved the engine on the strimmer, the squirrel appeared to huff in disgust and then disappeared among the leaves. After several minutes of searching for it, the children gave up and returned to their leaf collecting. Mr Parson began to attack the brambles.

Suddenly, a scream erupted from the young boy. "Snake!" he stammered, pointing in fear at the patch of ground he had just cleared. His sister just caught a glimpse of silver flash into the long grass – enough to recognise it as a slow worm and therefore comfort her younger brother. Once again, a few more minutes were spent trying to trace it for a closer look but once again, another creature had managed to escape them.

The leaf collection was now forgotten. The children were excited to explore the wilderness in search of more critters. Pulling aside creepers, weeds and fallen foliage revealed an array of mini-beasts and evidence of greater creatures such as nibble marks of rodents and the pungent aroma of a fresh fox scat! Each discovery was heralded with squeals of delight at the hidden treasures in their own garden.

Another screech suddenly echoed around the garden. This time a higher pitch, not human, but something altogether different. Mr Parson immediately silenced the strimmer and looked at the ground beneath him. Now all was quiet and a small trickle of blood could be seen beneath the debris. The children, pale faced, trembled as their father pushed aside the waste greenery. A small hedgehog lay damaged in the soil. The strimmer wire had cut cleanly across its back and had left little chance of survival for the poor creature. The family stood and watch it take its last breath.

Full of tears, the children buried the unfortunate victim beneath a beautiful shrub that had yet to suffer the fate of the clearance. Mr Parson solemnly locked the strimmer back in the shed and the family retreated to their house. The passion they had previously shown for their gorgeous garden, now forgotten.

After several days, the family were invited round to meet their new neighbours. The children enjoyed the company of the two young boys who lived next door. Eventually, the four of them decided to go outside to play. The neighbour's garden was a huge expanse of flat lawn, almost manicured, despite the scars of many kick-abouts and scuffles. Looking around, the Parsons' children were shocked at the sterility of it all. Thinking back to their unfortunate hedgehog, they longed to be back in their own backyard jungle and once again treasure hunting within it.

When they returned home, the family sat around the table discussing the events of the past few days. It would seem that they all held the same view of the barren expanse next door, compared to their own wild paradise.

The next few days passed in a flurry of calls, emails and visits to the local wildlife trust, the council's tree officer and various other nature experts. With the strimmer still locked in the shed, Mr Parsons brandished a pair of loppers and carefully tidied the more wild areas of the garden. One corner, overrun with nettles, was left alone to attract butterflies. The silver birches remained standing, following a quick trim of their dead branches, and the lawn was cleared enough for a space to play but with a healthy edging of shrubs to provide shelter for the other residents of the property.

Finally, it seemed, flora, fauna and families could reside in harmony in their small patch of urban utopia.

Carolyn Hide, Primary Teacher, Hampshire.

The following story represents a future generation. One, that I hope, will help to save this planet and its wildlife from the problems we have caused.

Harliv Dhuria, Aged 9, Hampshire.

SAVE THE DOLPHINS

In the depths of the ocean, live the rarely spotted Maui dolphins. They have a rounded dorsal fin and live in groups. As the groups are sex segregated, the males are separate from the females and calves. This group was of females and calves. The calves were playing, darting in and out of the coral. The females were busy looking for food with which they would feed themselves and their youngsters. The oldest calf was three years of age and her name was Alicia. She had a brother named Alex who was one. Their friends were Brittany, Dora and Finlay who were all two years old.

The calves were playing hide and seek, and Dora was counting when a fishing net trawled over the dolphins' home. Dora screamed and hid, along with everyone else. Alicia and Alex didn't know that there was a net above them, so they came out. WHAM!! They were swept up by the net and captured.

Alicia woke up with a start. Where was she? Alex was next to her, also awake. Suddenly, they heard a booming noise. They also heard a, "What did we catch?" Another noise was heard.

"You should see this for yourself."

The pair of dolphins were terrified. Some small and skinny men peered from above. To Alicia and Alex, they were aliens. A huge man strode in. He took one look at the dolphins and nearly fainted.

"My goodness!" He exclaimed. "They are Maui dolphins, extremely rare sea animals."

Everyone was taken aback.

"Should we release them sir," asked another man. This made the boss think for a second.

"No," he replied, "we will keep them".

'Oh no!' thought the dolphins, who were listening attentively. They were carted off to a big room which was full of tanks. They

87

were all full to the brim with water. Alex had only seen one big tank and thought it was the sea.

"Oh goody!" exclaimed Alex elatedly, "They are taking us somewhere near home." But Alicia had seen all the tanks and knew better.

"Alex," she said in a terrified voice, "I think we are going to be trapped in an aquarium."

Alex didn't understand the meaning of that.

"What's an aquarium?" asked Alex confused. Alicia was so shocked that she almost forgot to explain it to him.

"An aquarium," replied Alicia when she came to her senses, "is a place where fish and other sea animals are trapped. We might not see mum and our friends ever again."

Just then, they were put in an empty tank which was for Dolphins only. Alicia noticed that they were the biggest animals there and as soon as they were on their own, Alex started to explore. As he took everything in, he bumped his head on the wall. Alicia went to him and bumped her head too. The boss just happened to be passing and noticed that the dolphins were hurt. He started panicking.

'They must be put in the sickness tank,' he thought. So, he put them there. But what the boss didn't know was that there was a hole, which acted as a drain. Alicia spotted it as she was being put in the tank.

'The drain is wide enough,' thought Alicia and if the pair went in single file, there would still be space around them. Alicia had a plan.

Every night, the boss did an inspection. If he caught any fish trying to escape, he would take it out of the water for 5 minutes, but Alicia felt brave and said to Alex, "Wait there. I'm going down the drain."

A quarter of an hour later, she reached the sea. She quickly sought out Brittany and told her the plan she had made.

I have come down to tell you my plan. I need you to find my distant cousin, Daisy. Tell her to do an eye- catching routine to the humans. Then me and Alex, along with the other fish with us, will escape. The humans will try to catch Daisy and fail, so everyone will be safe."

Brittany swam off to tell the other dolphins. Alicia went back to the others in the aquarium. She told the others of her plan then wondered aloud 'How was she going to get the other fish down the drain?'

An octopus offered to pull the tanks next to each other so the fish could jump from one tank to another. The plan was put into action. Strangely, there was a window behind the dolphins' tank so that they could see the sea. Alicia's mum went to look for Daisy.

Daisy was a Baiji dolphin, and they were extremely rare too. At 8pm sharp, Daisy did her tricks, which were baffling. She did her routine which included a triple front flip in the air, a double spin and then the ultimate quadruple back flip in the air. The humans saw it and came rushing with their nets. Alicia and Alex saw this and knew it was their cue.

In preparation for the journey, Alicia used her echolocation to tell the fish the way to get to the sea. They dove down to the path, which was twisty, dark and damp, but they still kept going.

In just five minutes, they reached the sea and as the drain ended, each fish could see some of their family members there. Finlay had alerted all the families of the homecoming fish. They were overjoyed and rushed to the scene. All animals were welcomed with celebration and laughter but most of all, they were welcomed with love.

There was a feast and joy returned to the ocean. However, joy was not everywhere. The humans were very angry because they failed to catch Daisy and the fish that they had already caught were now free. But as far as this story goes, all was well.

46586606R00061

Printed in Poland
by Amazon Fulfillment
Poland Sp. z o.o., Wrocław